the harbingers

bhikkhu sujato

20/1/2022

First edition: 2022

Creative Commons Zero (CC0 1.0 Universal)
To the extent possible under law, the author Bhikkhu Sujato has waived all copyright and related or neighboring rights to *The Harbingers* and dedicates it to the public domain. Please take this and do whatever you want with it.

ISBN: 978-1-921842-27-6

Lovingly crafted with pandoc, Visual Studio Code, and Ubuntu. Typeset in Crimson Pro.

Cover image "Out of the Pyro" used with kind permission of the photographer, Paul McIver.

Published by The Publisher at the End of the World.

the
harbingers

bhikkhu sujato

There can be no keener revelation of a society's soul than the way in which it treats its children. — Nelson Mandela

contents

preface i

prologue 1

before the dissolution 13

   strike squad five—attack! 14

   the far side of the sky (1) 20

   just a kid 22

   the far side of the sky (2) 26

   blame it on the sunshine 28

   the far side of the sky (3) 32

   choices 33

   the far side of the sky (4) 38

   language 39

   the far side of the sky (5) 55

   t-shirts 58

   the far side of the sky (6) 61

   just the basic facts 64

the far side of the sky (7)   78

the town hall   82

after the dissolution   **93**

to cast a light in hidden places   94

the other chris   103

the possession of a uterus   107

in the presence of ghosts   111

unusually rich soil   116

an efficient solution   124

the dry wanted breaking   129

gods and monsters   132

the marsh's edge   137

on fire they descended   139

norm   149

epilogue   **167**

timeline   **171**

preface

Do you ever get the feeling that the future sometimes slips into the present? Like, you look over there and see something that is not but may yet come to be? Perhaps the present simply gets tired and lets the mask slip. It's probably nothing. Anyway, I wrote down a few of these fugitive glimpses and ended up with a book.

The story of the Buddha follows the outlines of the classical hero myth: going forth into the wilderness to overcome monsters (of the psychological and spiritual variety, of course) and win a great prize. Mendicants used to emulate this by wandering through the jungle from village to village. But now the forests are pretty much gone, and if they wander at all, it is along dusty bitumen highways.

The whole hero's journey thing is super blokey. It was Marina Warner's *From the Beast to the Blonde* that taught me how women told a different kind of story: how to vanquish the hairy monster in the bedroom. It seemed to me that stories like *Beauty and the Beast*, *Little Red Riding Hood*, and especially *Bluebeard* lay the template for the modern horror story, where the monster is inside the house and the aim is not to win a prize, but simply to get out alive.

Now the age of heroes is over. They killed the monsters and

tamed the wilderness, domesticating the whole world. We thought this would make us safe. Turns out, the monsters were inside the house all along.

Climate change, AI, the creeping decay of democracy: most of us expend quite a bit of effort maintaining the polite fiction that this is all quite normal. Some call it denial, others coping. But I wonder: what kind of people might we become, were we to stop pretending?

———————————

Content warning: Members of Aboriginal and Torres Strait Islander communities are advised that this work of fiction contains names of deceased First Nations peoples.

In this book, I represent several stories, events, and ideas as Aboriginal. I am not an Aboriginal person, and these are not my stories. They should not be taken as reliable or accurate representations of the lives and culture of First Nations peoples. I reflect on them to make sense of my story. If there is any fault in my representation, I ask forgiveness.

This story was largely written on the unceded land of the Burramattagal people. I pay respects to those people and their elders past, present, and emerging.

This is not a book for young children. It contains potentially distressing content such as:

- apocalypse
- strong language
- poetry

Many thanks are due to Bhikkhu Akaliko, with whom I tested the first drafts of many chapters; and to Alex Neville, Vanessa Sasson, and Bhikkhu Sumano, who gave valuable feedback on an earlier draft. And special thanks to all those who have supported my monastic life with generosity and kindness.

The cover photo "Out of the Pyro" is by Paul McIver and is used with his kind permission. It was featured in the Head On Photo Festival, the Walkley Foundation digital photojournalism exhibition, "The summer Australia burned, 2019–2020", and the Black Summer exhibition at the Magnet Galleries, Melbourne.

Here is the story behind the photo.

> The first fire I photographed this season was in August 2019. There was snow in the background! As the season wore on the fires became more frequent until the pyro cumulonimbus event of New Year's Eve generated by the Badja and Good Good fires around Numeralla. This fire would later claim the air tanker. Midday looked like midnight, but no one was celebrating. No one had ever seen anything like it before as day was turned to night and a sense of foreboding descended with the cloud of ash and smoke.

> We drove for over fifteen kilometres into this event, with lightning striking around us intermittently, before losing our nerve and turning around to follow those fleeing

back out. This image was taken as we exited the event. I went on to file occasionally for the Sunday Telegraph in Sydney in the weeks and months ahead. Exactly a month later an offshoot of this fire destroyed my home of 30 plus years. No one has seen such times before. If I could ask but one thing it would be, can we please start being kinder to our mother!"

prologue

Between the mountains and the sea there lay a wide valley by a narrow river. There the salt water mixed with the fresh and eels born in distant seas came to lie down in the mangroves.

Many years ago, people made their home there. They became known as the Burramattagal people of the Dharug nation. They fished and foraged and fought and farted and made love beneath the stars, and they sang the story of their ancestors in the long years of their Dreaming. In the sky above there shone a golden emu egg to warm their days and light their path. Ever changing, ever adapting, they cultivated the region into a great garden, full of fruit and fish. They made paths that linked the peoples of the rivers and the inlets, down to the ocean and up to the mountains, on to the plains beyond, and even to the endless desert of the interior.

In time, they gained a friend: the dingo, a fierce hunter and a playful companion. Women suckled dingo pups, who in turn gave warmth and protection. But they always went back to their wild ways. When times were hard and dry, the dingo could always lead you to water.

They took their canoes out on the waters and lit fires on them.

There were few sights more beautiful than the canoes out at night, their sparkling flames reflecting off the Sydney waters under the starry sky. By their homes on the shores, they cast their discarded shellfish in heaps. As the millennia went by, the heaps grew to be vast middens towering over their heads, a slow testimony to their long stewardship.

In their stories the land was a living thing, full of magic and love and monsters. The stories did not live in books, but in the shine of the stars and the tang of the wattle and the sly glance of the quoll. Each story was a thread that wove the past into the future. Their world sparkled with such threads, so that everywhere you looked was rich with meaning.

After a very long time, something happened that was not in any of the stories. Something that threatened the life of the people.

Strangers came to the shores in big boats. They had disturbingly white skin; a ridiculous arrangement, as it burned red in the sun and peeled off in sheets. Their skin was so useless, they had to wear another skin on top of it! Despite their fragility, the strangers invaded the land and remained. They made a camp in the cove they called Sydney. Upstream, a day's walk from Sydney, they made a farming settlement on the river. Taking the language of the people, they named it Parramatta.

The invaders demonstrated no culture, no sense of place. They showed no respect to the people or their laws. They described the landscape as a truly beautiful park, filled with an endless variety of hill and dale, clothed in the most luxuriant herbage, rich in soil and wildlife, through which a person on a horse might easily gallop in any direction beneath the stately trees. They did not understand that this was no raw state of nature, but the outcome of millennia of gentle, careful management and cultivation. So they took what they wanted and peered at the people like specimens. There was a wariness between the people and the invaders; and soon enough, it turned bloody.

In the face of increasingly violent attacks, the people fought to protect their home. The warrior Pemulwuy marched into Parramatta at the head of a hundred strong men with spears. But the white men had guns. They killed many and wounded Pemulwuy, but he escaped. So the Governor issued an order that any Aboriginals in Parramatta be shot on sight. Spurred by a reward, men hunted Pemulwuy down and killed him. They cut off his head and sent it to England for science. Much later, they named a suburb after him.

It never really occurred to the invaders that they might have something to learn from the people who had lived there for thousands of years. To them, the Aboriginals were no more than brutes.

Instead of learning, they took it upon themselves to teach the First Peoples their language, the values and ways that they had brought with them from far distant lands. A Burramattagal girl named Boorong was one of their cleverest pupils. One night, Boorong came to the white folk full of agitation and terror, foretelling a great doom. She had seen a falling star and knew what it portended. No-one knew what to make of this distraught girl and her odd ravings. Laughing, they shooed her away. But some days later, a messenger arrived from the Sydney Cove settlement bearing a disturbing report. The flagship HMS *Sirius* had run aground at Slaughter Bay on Norfolk Island. There was no loss of life, but its wreckage deprived the starving colony of a vital supply ship. When they heard this report, they remembered what Boorong had said. No-one knew what to make of it.

That was not the only disaster to befall the invaders. For many years it was touch and go. For all their fancy duds and put-on graces, the white folk were a messy lot. They squabbled among themselves, traded in rum, and every other year they nearly starved. But soon enough they paved the paths and struck down the ancient middens, grinding them into lime for mortar. They cut the bones of the earth into squares and, piling them one on top of the other, made tall buildings, glued together with the paste of ancient shellfish.

It was hard work for many years, but the white people managed to chop down almost all the trees. They were nothing if not industrious. No matter how tall the trees were, how strong the roots and stubborn, they just wouldn't give up. It was who they were—conquerors of nature.

Like the First Peoples—like all peoples in fact—the white folk were shaped in profound ways by their past; or more to the point, by the stories they told themselves about their past. What transfixed them more than anything else was the story of *dominion*. They were lords; the world was to be lorded over. Nature existed for them, its only purpose the service of their desires. To that end, they did not hesitate to strip, crush, and rend, reshaping the world until it took on a new form designed for their comfort and convenience.

The story of dominion was old. So old, they had forgotten where it came from. To them, it had always been there. It informed their culture and views so deeply, they could not understand that there might be other ways of knowing. But any story has a beginning, and the oldest story of dominion that we know of dates from nearly 5,000 years ago. It survived in fragments told and retold over thousands of years, carefully pieced together and deciphered by experts from broken clay tablets of Sumer and Babylon. It tells of the first hero, Gilgamesh.

Gilgamesh was a great king of the city of Uruk. To magnify his glory and ensure his eternal fame, he enlisted his friend Enkidu in a mad quest. He proposed to venture into the great cedar forest of Lebanon for wood to build his city. The hills of Lebanon, through which flowed the river Jordan, were covered in magnificent trees, strong enough to build for a thousand years.

But the forest was not defenseless. It was guarded by Humbaba, a fierce spirit with a broad flat nose, stripes painted on his face, big lips, and big teeth flashing out on dark skin.

Those set on plunder called him a monster, whose voice was the deluge, whose speech was fire, and whose breath was death. But not so the creatures of his own land. To them, he was the one who kept the paths clean and smooth, in whose honor the wood pigeons cooed and the turtle doves sweetly sang, while the mother monkeys chatted with their young beneath the fragrant ancient trees.

Gilgamesh assigned the duties of the city to stewards, then set out for Lebanon together with Enkidu. They journeyed in stages across seven mountain ranges. When they made camp in the evenings, Gilgamesh would invoke his gods, begging them to send him dreams to guide him. But his gods sent no auspicious signs, only portents of terror and desolation: mountains crumbling, storms crashing, wild bulls snorting, and a great bird breathing thunder and fire. Dismayed and fearful, he was soothed by Enkidu, who exhorted him to go on.

Finally they reached the forest, where they soon heard the mighty roar of Humbaba. Realizing that he could not best the giant in battle, Gilgamesh approached with a smile and the promise of gifts. He kissed the great being on the cheek. By the time Humbaba discerned his murderous intent, it was too late and he could only beg for mercy. He went so far as to offer Gilgamesh his service, to supply him with all the timber he needed. Gilgamesh hesitated; but, urged on by Enkidu, he sealed his glorious victory by sliding a sharp blade into Humbaba's neck. He murdered the spirit of the forest and stole the wood for his own, and that is how he became a hero. Humbaba's dying scream echoed through the forest, cursing Gilgamesh and Enkidu and all their works.

The story of Gilgamesh may have been forgotten, but its lesson was not. To find glory and everlasting fame, you must begin by murdering nature's protectors and don't forget to do it with a smile.

With their ancient guardian gone, the cedar forests were open to all. The list of those who consumed the cedar reads like a litany of ancient empire: Assyria, Babylon, Egypt, Phoenicia, Israel, Persia, Rome, Arabia. Not even the decree of the emperor Hadrian could stop the plunder.

Much later, the Ottoman Turks found a new use for the famously tough and durable timber: laying railroads. Then the English finished off all but a few stands in that absurd barbarism that we call World War I. But by that time they had already found an excellent new source of timber on the far side of the world.

The English came to Australia to fulfill a mission, the mission of civilization. Like Gilgamesh, they invoked the protection of their

God. They never questioned their task. They found a land covered with endless leagues of tall trees and they set to work. They cut down enough forest to cover France, Spain, and Germany combined.

The people of the land noticed an odd thing about the strangers. Some of them wore bright-colored clothes and lived in big buildings. They seemed to get all the good things. But they were not the ones doing the work; they just yelled and told people what to do. Other white folk, dressed in rags and bound in chains, spent all day breaking rocks or levelling ground, but for all their hard work they slept behind bars and ate grey sludge.

It seemed an unfair way to arrange things: the land and the sky were ample and abundant, why could not all share equally? But no: big men lived in big buildings while little people squatted in little hovels. They were only allowed in the big houses to clean or cook.

Bigger still than the houses of the big men were the houses of the law. The biggest of all was the house they built for an old white man called God. They called it St Johns after a man in their stories named John the Baptist. But the funny thing was, he himself would never have lived in such a place. The invaders idolized him, but in truth, he was nothing like them.

John was a brown-skinned man who lived about two thousand years ago in the land of Lebanon. It was a long time ago, but still thousands of years after Gilgamesh had opened that country up for felling the cedar. By John's time, millennia of logging had decimated the vast tracts of lush forest, and the land had grown barren and desolate. It was to these deserts that John retreated in search of wisdom; to him, the desert was the state of nature. There he lived, much like the Burramattagal, on locusts and wild honey.

After many years, he came in from the wilderness to proclaim the redemption of sin. It was never exactly clear what sin he came to redeem; but perhaps that did not matter so very much, for must we not all be guilty of something? He took his people from the hot sands and blessed them in the cool waters of the river Jordan.

A man came to John and knelt before him, saying, "I have wandered for so long now on paths grievous and strange. I am lost, and cannot recall all I have done along the way. But I do know this: my crimes are many. I have hurt the ones I love and forsaken the path of righteousness. These hands were given so that I may serve, but with them I have dealt only death. My lips were given so that I may speak the truth, but my lies have led many down false paths. Take me to your river. Drown me in your sweet waters. In your arms, let the river wash my sins away, so that I may know what it is to rise once more, free at last from all my burdens."

John took that man in his strong arms, sinner and criminal though he was, and blessed him in the river. The river cared not who entered its waters; it washed them all alike.

Like Boorong of the Burramattagal clan, John had the sight, or so it would seem. He told of one who would come, far greater than he, a savior and redeemer of his people. Perhaps it was this that the the settlers of Parramatta were thinking of when they named their church St Johns. The white folk liked to imagine themselves as saviors of the First People. "Before we came they had nothing," they said.

But one who entered that house of cold stone would find no savior there. There was only a pale dull man wrapped in dark cloth and solemn countenance, muttering incantations in a foreign tongue.

They called him the "Flogging Parson" due to his penchant for flailing the flesh of young bodies into quivering jelly. He cast spells infusing plain bread with the living spirit of his god, then he devoured it. It was in this way that he broke the magic of the land that he disdained as primitive. He believed that his obscure rites and ancient tomes made him worthy to decree for all what was right and what was wrong. From his high pulpit, the Flogging Parson declared that the First People were the most degraded form of the human race.

Facing St Johns church they built the Town Hall, where big men got together and made rules for the little people to live by. Nearby were the courts, where they judged the little people by the rules they had made, and the prisons, where they locked them up. Plenty of the First People found themselves on the wrong side of these new laws and ended up inside a prison cell. In those cells, sitting still and gazing up at the little barred window, their dreaming grew dim and faded into shadows.

The white folk were full of disease. They infected the people with sicknesses that rotted their skin or stole their breath. Most of them died. When the white folk died, they were buried in the cemetery near St Johns, their lives marked in stone. But the Burramattagal were granted no such honor; fractured or dispersed, the story of the land was taken from them. Their only witness was silence.

Against all odds, the colony survived and grew. Sydney became famous for its beaches and its Opera House on the harbor, a shining city on the sea. Parramatta grew along with it, becoming Sydney's biggest satellite. It was never exactly fashionable or particularly bustling, but it certainly had a Westfields. On a Friday evening, greasy white boys hooned around in lime Monaros blasting *Highway to Hell*, while women on their way home from the office sat uneasily at lonely bus stops.

Over the years, the fish-and-chip shops selling chiko rolls were replaced by streetside cafés selling quinoa salad and cappuccinos. Friday night's entertainment was supplied by greasy brown boys pumping doof doof and chucking blockies in a WRX. Fancy shiny offices sprang up, their aspirational glass mirroring the *For Lease* sign next door.

The old Town Hall saw it all: the happy-clappers spruiking for converts, the leathery bogans with their mullets and DBs, the kids waving signs that protested, "There's no planet B!"

But the white folk had no room in their new world for the people of the land. They were writing their own story of progress and success, of dominion, and in their story they were the heroes. They made sure that those who called themselves Burramattagal were killed or scattered, chased into the shadows. The old stories faded away, and with them the memory of what it was like before.

It's tempting to see this as a sign, a harbinger if you will. But harbingers are a tricky thing. What does it mean that Boorong, the name of the girl who saw doom in a falling star, meant "star" in the language of the Burramattagal? Or that the ship whose doom she foresaw, the *Sirius*, was named for the brightest star in the sky?

The thing is, the events themselves don't mean anything: they just happened. It is humans who feel the need to read meaning into patterns, to turn coincidence into synchronicity, to turn a sequence of events into a narrative. Perhaps it is because we feel the loss of the old stories that once traced meaning in the stars and the stones. Everywhere we look we see a universe indifferent to us, and so we

10

grasp at ersatz mysteries, losing ourselves in the merest surface of words.

It's only natural to want to belong, to find meaning. But here's the problem. The death of a people is not like the falling of a star. It is a tragedy in itself, not a sign of a tragedy to come. It does not exist to give meaning to *our* lives. It has no meaning, no moral; it is the breaking of meaning, the breaking of morality. There is no morality that can account for the death of all things. Faced with the consequences of humanity's deeds, what are we to do? March as warriors shaking sharp spears, or surrender to the quiet waters?

Our moralities lie broken and bleeding, whimpering echoes of the days of surety. Today, the river Jordan is choked and poisoned, a sickly trickle of sewage, agricultural runoff, and industrial filth. Not despite the fact that it flows through an ancient sacred land, but because of it. Once we went into it to wash away our sins, but our sins grew so great they killed the river. Now there is no place on this broad earth free from the stain of human sin.

Anyway, at the time, no-one hardly noticed. The dead could not speak, or if they could, their voices were drowned out by the clamour of the living. The dead were gone, and who would begrudge the living their chance at a good life? Were they meant to live out their days in sorrow for the sins of their ancestors? There would be plenty of time for sorrow. Meanwhile it was time to live, and live they did.

For a while, it was possible to imagine Parramatta as a place of vitality and renewal.

For a while, it was possible to imagine.

For a while.

before the dissolution

strike squad five—attack!

"Strike Squad Five!" barked Sharon. "Attack! Attack!"

"Jesus, dial it back a notch," said Mags. "Give it a minute."

"Do you have any idea the kind of destruction that thing can wreak in a minute?" came the retort. "Strike Squad Five! Attack! Oh, never mind, too late, it's gone." She picked up her pet goanna and snuggled it, nuzzling it to her big sister's disgust. "Who's a widdle wazybones then? Too fat? Too full? Don't wanna chase the mousy?"

"Ew gross, get a room," laughed Mags.

"Scoff all you like," said Sharon, "but I'm getting hotter action than you."

"You're not wrong," sighed Mags. "But still, you're crazy if you think that thing will catch one of the little bastards."

Sharon laid back, her head on Mags' legs as they sat in the grass. Strike Squad Five lolled uselessly nearby, his putative role as mouse-hunter neglected.

The sisters were joking around, but the mice were no joke. They were a plague, overrunning much of the farming land that stretched out west of Sydney. Two lazy teenagers and their even lazier pet goanna were proving as useless as all the other efforts to contain them. No matter what was done, still they came in their thousands from holes in the ground, from wheat silos, creeping up the walls, devouring and scampering and scraping.

These mice weren't native to Australia, of course. They came on the ships. They were always around, but now they had got out of control. And just when things had turned for the good, too. For the last few years, farmers had really struggled with drought. Turns out, the dry wasn't just bad for growing crops, it also killed off the birds and snakes who had been eating the mice. Now at last things were looking up with a wet, mild summer. Perfect for a bumper harvest, and also perfect breeding season for mice, with plenty of food in the fields and the silos, and few predators to keep them in check.

It was evening, the sun was setting, dogs were barking, and dinner was calling. They climbed up to the verandah and a couple of mice scampered off. Sharon didn't even bother to put SS5 down to chase them. She just put him gently to bed in his little cage.

Dinner was heaping on the table as the family gathered. When little Donny ran in, Mags said, "Shut up, Donny!"

"What!" he protested, "I didn't say anything!"

"And now you've gone and ruined it," she teased. Sharon giggled, but she tousled her little brother's head as he sat down.

They sat around the table, chatting and giggling. Mum was warm and giving, taking care of everyone, asking all the questions. Despite her best efforts, there was a mouse or two scurrying around her kitchen.

Dad was quiet as always, communicating mostly in grunts. Nothing wrong, just he was tired is all. It was hard enough to work a farm in the best of days, and this was not that, what with the financials and the heat. And now on top of everything else, he was spending an hour or more morning and evening laying water-traps and poison, and clearing away the stench of dead rodents. It wasn't what he signed up for.

That night, Sharon found a dead mouse on her pillow. No big deal, just get rid of it like the rest. But it struck her, lying there; it was actually cute in a way. What kind of life did it have? It was so sad.

The mouse didn't know it was a symptom of a collapsing ecosphere. It just lived, same as anything else. But did it have a soul? Where did it go when it died? Or did it just end? Is that all there was?

She brushed it into a pan—mice could carry diseases—and held it up for a look. Its little body was still warm and soft. She wondered why it died; it looked skinny. When the food ran short, they began eating each other. She thought of what it had been through in its short life and tears welled in her eyes. It was no pest, just a creature trying to live. But she needed sleep, so she tossed it out the window. There'd be more come sunup.

Sleep came slowly. It was never really quiet anymore; there was always a rustling and a scampering. It would die away for a second, then there'd be a scrabble and a squeak. It was like living inside the world's most horrifying ASMR video. And the smell! She couldn't remember her home ever being free of the stench of mouse.

She slept, and in her sleep a dream came to her.

She lay all in black upon land that was a blue-black scar, oily and slick, ravaged and barren. Inside her there was an insensate longing; a yearning that had no object and no end. In the distance a sun was rising, all purple fringed with red. The sun had a face, and in that face a baleful eye slowly opened and leered down upon a world of death and smoke and pain. Tormented wires writhed like snakes. Concrete choked on its own dust. Sickly grey-green blobs of slime jabbered and spat. She came to a swelling river, but could not cross the bridge. Underneath, the current was too strong. Then she tried climbing the pylons. Surprisingly, she found that she was easily able to ride her bicycle over the steel cables. The far shore was lush with grass. Beyond there was a shining palace, bright with jewelled

16

windows; but it was empty. In its forecourt there was a single tree, white and leafless, and upon its bough it bore a golden mango. She was happy there and lay down to rest in the grass. The prince, who had been with her all along, whispered in her ear, "Kiss me, my love, so that I may become a prince."

She woke to the feel of little feet crawling on her lips. Oh God, yuck, she spat. It ran off. She leapt up, groggy and spitting, shuddering in disgust. After rinsing her mouth she got back in bed, but sleep was no longer an option. She sat in the dark, surrounded by tiny creatures who were guilty of nothing but wanting to live. She took SS5 from his cage and cuddled him; they always kept each other company.

Next morning, they had some time after breakfast, so the girls got Donny to come play cricket. There was a makeshift pitch out back, not far from the house.

"Howzat!" yelled Mags, as her ball flew ridiculously wide. Donny just shook his head in despair. "Alright, whatever, this time it'll be different!" she said. But sadly it was not to be.

Sharon had put Strike Squad Five near the bush on the far side, away from the house. He seemed happy enough, getting a little morning sun. The kids played happily.

But was that something? A sound, maybe? Yes, a sound. "Hey, what's up?" said Donny, as the two girls grew still and listened. It was deep like the ocean.

"What the hell is that?" said Sharon. "It's getting louder." They'd not heard anything like this before, and they had lived their whole lives on this property.

A mouse ran out of the bushes near SS5, who just looked at it. But it ran like the devil itself was after it. Then came another, then a group, then a wave of mice.

"Ahh no, this is getting ..." said Mags.

"Hey, Strike Squad Five, c'mon," called Sharon, stepping over to grab her pet. But the mice erupted. Over, under, and through the bush, they burst like a tsunami, the whole place suddenly boiling over with billions of the creatures. Sharon screamed as they swarmed over the goanna. Donny ran; Mags grabbed Sharon's hand and they ran too, seeking the relative safety of the verandah. The three kids looked back in terror, seeing the yard overrun. Where Strike Squad Five was, there was just a roil of mice, devouring.

But that wasn't the end of it—the mice were right behind them. The first wave was already climbing the steps, up the posts, making for the windows and doors. The kids were really panicking now, this was just too much, where could they hide? Just then, Dad appeared. On his back he had a flamethrower. All the farmers had them these days, and this was the reason why.

"Out of the way!" he yelled, and standing at the top of the steps, he let rip. The fire swept out across the yard. As it torched the little creatures they screeched in agony. Mice were fried in their thousands, reduced to a writhing mass of tormented critters, their fur ablaze, squealing and struggling to escape. Still they came, wave upon wave of living beings. Some got through, but most ended up charred meat, fur, and bone. The air filled with the unearthly shrieking of half-dead rodents, rising in a howl above the roar of the flame. As the whole yard filled with fire, the oncoming wave shied off, dividing itself into two streams, either side of the house, flowing like a flood from who-knows-where to who-goddamn-cares.

The kids stood there, shaking, as the mice passed. Dad stepped into the yard, sweeping the piled up bodies with fire, making sure they were all dead.

He kept going until the fuel ran out. The smell of petrol was everywhere, and underneath was a note of charred meat like a barbecue. The job was done, the mice were gone, the day was saved. Everyone was safe. Everyone was okay. It was fine. But when he looked up at his kids, there was horror in his eyes. He hated that they saw him like this. A family was for love and joy, not fire and burnt flesh. What the hell were they doing? What kind of world was this for a child?

"Go inside, kids," he said. "I'll clean up the yard."

Still in shock, they fumbled for the door. But Sharon paused. She turned and said, "It's okay, Dad. We'll help. Guys, let's get the fire-rakes."

the far side of the sky (1)

Hi dad,

How are you? I am good. This is the address you told me to use, I hope it gets to you!

School is good. Jason ate a snail.

When are you coming home? Sometimes I don't sleep good. I miss your beard.

Arixys

My dear Arixys,

Namaste! My dearest child, I pray that you are well. ("Well", not "good"! If you say you are "good", you mean that you are a morally upright person!)

Please don't fret. I know it is strange to have me away like this, but I promise there is a good reason. All will be made clear in good time.

Does it sometimes feel like each day is a step in the wrong direction? Like the news is full of dire warnings and dreary portent? Like you try to stay positive, but the world is against you? Yes? Well, you are not alone, for I know exactly how that feels!

What if I were to tell you, my beloved Arixys, that here, at the end of all hope, it is joy unlooked-for that fills my heart? Would you believe me? It matters not, for soon you shall see for yourself. I have learned a great truth: we are safe. It turns out, our Leaders have had a plan all along. We can stop worrying; we'll be fine.

Not the earth, though. It is tragic, but we can no longer deny the all-too-obvious truth: the planet is done for. But that should not distress us overly much, for what matters is us. Nature and animals are very nice, of course, but they are not invested with value in and of themselves. We are the ones who are conscious and awake, who contain the seeds of enlightenment, and who can take responsibility for our actions. Those actions, admittedly, include killing trillions of animals and wiping out millions of species, wreaking havoc and devastation at a scale that no other creature could rival. But it is we humans who have the unique capacity to reflect on our mistakes, to feel sorry for them, and to hope to do better in the future.

I cannot say too much. But let me venture this: be not afraid, for our fates rest safe in strong and capable hands.

Yours in hope,

Edgar

just a kid

In a suburb thousands of miles away on the far side of the continent sat a teenage boy, bored out of his mind on a hot Saturday arvo. The grownups were having a barbie, but he was off in his own world.

It was such a small thing. Very common. Not the first and surely not the last. He looked closely, taking in each detail. An irregular shape. A firmness. A faint tackiness to the touch. A feeling of almost pain.

Somehow this thing was born out of a rupture, where what was supposed to be whole was sundered. Yet healing required no intervention. He could just forget about it and the wholeness would come into being.

"Were all things like this?" he pondered. Was wholeness the state of nature and we only observers? Or is this a characteristic of life only? Things generally seemed to go the other way. Crumbling was their nature. Didn't matter if you were a brick or a spaceship, a piece of carpet or a mountain, your every second was falling apart.

But life though. It broke that rule. It got better. It organized itself. Is that what life is? Self-organizing structures, always moving from the simple to the complex, scoffing at entropy?

But that takes energy. It isn't magic, there's no special vital force. It's about information, coding information in DNA, sets of instructions for unfolding complex organic unities from ternary codes. Energy has to be funnelled from chaos and shaped into form.

And here he was—whoa! He was the end result of all that and he was *thinking about it*! His mind curled back as he reached a point where there seemed no footing. How could he think about thinking about thinking? It seemed impossible. He tried for a while and gave up. He wondered. How is it? How is the world built this way? Is it so that we can never find the key? What would happen if we did? What would the key unlock? Would it be wonderful, or would the whole thing just unravel?

"Uggh, yuk!" interrupted his mother. "Chris! Stop picking at your scab!"

"I wasn't," he lied.

The grownups laughed. "Okay then, sure."

He was ashamed to be doing something so childlike. Well, ashamed to be caught. And annoyed: his reverie was over. And vaguely contemptuous: there they were, drinking beer, laughing about sports. Shouldn't grownups be better, wiser? Maybe they were, but they sure hid it. They seemed so stupid. Just going about their lives as if the world wasn't ending.

He leaped up and went outside. Hopping on his bike, he spun down the street, jumping gutters and kerbs. Sweat poured off him, but he pumped the pedals even harder. He came out, as he knew he would, dodging through a secret alley into a wide open road. It was an abandoned construction project, supposed to be a new suburb. But the money ran out; no-one was buying. So there was nothing to stop him as he sped down the hill, faster and faster, the broad smooth road offering no check. There'd been a birdfall; he couldn't dodge the little bodies: bumpity-splat they went under his wheels. The wind dried his sweat and the speed felt good. It whipped thought from his mind.

He was getting near the bottom. The unfinished road stopped abruptly in a tangle of barriers and parked machinery. Closer and closer, challenging himself every time. There it was, the line from last time, a skid on the brand-new tarmac. He kept going, crossed the line, then jammed the brakes as hard as he could. He skidded and careened at a barrier, almost missing, but then smashing into it at the last moment. He tumbled off the bike, took a few turns, and ended up lying face down, panting and laughing. Oh yeah, that was fun. And yep, there'll be another scab tomorrow.

Picking himself up, he got back on his bike and kept going. More sedately this time, as he was near the bottom of the slope. Turning off the construction site, he picked his way along a narrow dirt path through a patch of bush. It led down to the water, his own secret place. Just a short turn from the crowds and concrete, here there was just nature.

From his pocket he pulled a pack of Twisties and ripped it open. Munching, he opened his notebook and sat for a while, then he wrote down his words.

> was there anyone who ever knew
> how the shags hung out their wings to dry?
> how the soft mud shelved so gradually
> beneath the perfect sky?
>
> what was the secret that he sought
> in yellowed grass, in tepid brine
> or in that soggy salt-flat smell
> where jellyfish lay dying?
>
> when skin is shed, what pink is left?
> what moisture is not soothing?

had he a thought what this was worth,
the summer he was losing?

he never lacked for warmth or love
but did he really care for such?
or was his heart already drifting
out into the marsh?

The sun drew low over the roughs and the reeds. As he got up to leave, he noticed a little worm, turned up in the soft mud, wriggling its way back into the soil. He thought to help it, but then, it seemed to be doing fine all on its own. So he left it.

Carelessly, he chucked the empty Twisties packet. He was just a kid after all.

the far side of the sky (2)

Dear dad,

Hi, I got your letter. I don't really understand. I wish things would go back to normal. They closed school again. Jason died.

There are lots of fires and smoke. I'm scared.

Arixys

Dear Arixys,

So sorry to hear about Jason. Did you have a funeral? Don't worry, we'll find you something even better than a puppy, I promise!

Don't forget to meditate like I taught you. Breathe in, breathe out, focus on your breath. Concentrate! Don't think about anything else. Those things can only affect you if you let them. You can be happy if you choose! Fear is a choice, my darling, don't let it be yours.

I am fairly bursting! I have so much to tell you! Soon, I promise, I can say more. For now, let me just say this.

Look into the sky. Remember how I taught you to spot our neighbors, Mars and Venus, when it is night? About how, as beautiful as they look, Mars is cold and desolate, and Venus is a horrible place of acid and fire? You know how we talked about space, and travelling to the stars? About how science fiction is not the same as reality? How other worlds, the ones we know of, are harsh and unforgiving, and it is crazy to think about colonizing them when we have our own beautiful planet Earth? Now I want you to go outside. Go on! Look up, look to the sun. Not right at it, you'll burn your eyes! It's so bright, can we see past it? What might there be on the other side?

Remember how we would march, waving our signs and chanting, "There's no Planet B"?

(What if we were wrong?)

In barely-contained excitement,

your loving father,

Edgar

blame it on the sunshine

Time went by and things fell apart. The boy called Chris who picked his scab grew up, travelled east, and went to med school to learn about life and healing, and forget about poetry and wonder. And in another suburb, not far away, another story unfolded of another life, with another man, who rather inconveniently was also called Chris. This Chris, it seems, was a bit upset.

"Get off-a my lawn!" he yelled, the sound jarring on the quiet suburban street. "You get off of it right now, y'hear?"

He was standing on the front lawn, watering it with a hose, as a woman stepped on to his property. He aimed the hose at the startled woman, who dodged the wet, mostly. But she didn't get off the lawn. She came right back at him, business suit be damned, pushing him back a few paces.

"Whad'ya mean, 'my' lawn," she demanded. "I think you mean, *our* lawn!"

"Oh yeah? And who put it down?" he rebutted convincingly. "Who weeds it? Who fertilizes it? Who is, even as we speak, watering it?"

"I don't know, maybe the one whose job was so slack he had the time to mess around playing with hoses?"

They locked glares for a minute, then he broke down and confessed, "Yes, your honor. I concede the case. Your logic is irrefutable. I throw myself at your feet. Have mercy on me, your serene magnificence!"

"Not a judge," she laughed. "But if I was, I'd find your shirtless ass guilty of being fine as hell, all shiny in the sunset like that."

28

"Well Cynthia,' he said, unembarrassed, "it's kinda warm, I dunno if you noticed. You know, in your fancy-schmancy lawyer office."

"And speaking of," she replied, "aren't we going to get fined? Didn't the water restrictions tighten up again?"

"They did," he said, "the tight bastards. But I've got ten minutes with the hose one evening a week, and by the grace of Bob Almighty, I'm bloody well going to use use it! My hose, my lawn, my water! A man is master of his own front yard! Until they take that away from me. They're probably watching right now, scheming."

"Now now, Chris," she said. "You can't blame it on the Council."

"Oh really?" he said, perking up. He knew where this was going.

"They're just people, doing their job. They're not to blame."

"Then who is to blame?" he grinned. "Who, dammit!"

"Well," she said, laughing, and jumped to the left. "Don't blame it on the sunshine!" When he turned the hose on her, she jumped back right. "Don't blame it on the moonlight!" And the hose turned again, settling into its rhythm. "Don't blame it on the good times!" And together they yelled, with more gusto than melody: "Blame it on the boogie!"

Holding each other, they began to twirl, the hose pointing up, shedding spirals of golden drops sparkling in the evening sun. "I just can't, I just can't, I just can't control my feet!"

And the water filled the air and rained down over the young happy couple as they danced and kissed in their own personal summer shower, spinning like Shiva in an ecstasy of joy and love and life.

29

And the water fell on the brown lawn and drained into the parched soil. Each drop of water sank into the earth, its viscosity drawing it around the grains of sand. It absorbed into the hair roots and refreshed the worms and the little creatures, binding the dust, giving life to the complex ecosystem underfoot. Soon, though, the trickle of water was too feeble to proceed; it penetrated only a few centimeters. And with the heat, even in the evening, it evaporated almost as rapidly as it flowed.

They didn't know it then. Or maybe they knew, they must've done, but they pushed it away. They were good people, kind and happy people, getting on with their lives. That's all. They weren't to blame.

But it didn't matter. When it came, it came for everyone. It was coming for them whether they knew it or not. Who cares if they were guilty? As far as the apocalypse was concerned, we were all guilty. It was out for blood, and it didn't care whose. It all smelled the same.

———————————————

That night she conceived. She carried the baby to term, but as her time drew near, things started getting out of hand. There were fires, worse than usual, and smoke filled the air. Floods hit hard, as summer storms came in, one after the other. Weird, dry storms, they whipped massive waves over the shores, yet their rainless winds only fed the flames. Protests, again, put down with violence, again. Meanwhile, yet another pandemic came down and the hospitals overflowed, again. It was hard to recruit staff. Who'd want a career with a death sentence?

So she was nervous when she went to hospital, and it didn't help that that night, there was a containment breach. Shocked, she heard gunfire inside the hospital itself. This wasn't America, what the hell were they doing with guns? With the nerves and the smoke, she had a panic attack with her contractions. The nurses were exhausted and distracted, the equipment unmaintained and faulty. They didn't notice the bad readings until too late.

Chris kept on saying, "Don't fret, they'll be here soon. This is a good hospital." Maybe it was once. But by the time a nurse checked the readout, she just looked scared and rushed to find a doctor. None came and they never saw the nurse again. Neither mother nor baby made it till dawn.

the far side of the sky (3)

Dad,

Please come home! I am so scared! Janice went and I'm all alone. I don't know what to do. There are noises outside the house. Drums in the streets. They are coming. I don't know what to do. I miss Jason.

_____

Dear Arixys,

Be strong, it will all be clear soon. I am on my way. Stay safe. Don't answer the door until you hear my voice.

yours,

Dad.

choices

"Well, at least you get a choice, so fess up."

"Oh my god, don't!"

"But I want to."

Sharon laughed. Her big sister wouldn't let up.

"Who is it to be? Wayne or Cole? It's on tomorrow, you can't just wait forever. A girl has to make her mind up one day. Even you!"

"You know it doesn't even work like that, right? I mean, just because I choose one of them doesn't mean anything's gonna happen."

Mags just giggled and chomped another Jaffa. On the screen, the heroine leaped over an impossible chasm, landing in the middle of a group of dark-clad soldiers, who she promptly demolished. The sisters whooped, "Go, girl!" It was a silly adventure flick, but a fun diversion. The cinema was full, which, given the crappiness of the film, was probably a world first. But no-one was there for the story. It was hot outside and the kids were getting some relief in the aircon.

"Now, let's break it down. Cole has history. He's a jackass, everyone knows that. After what happened two summers ago? Please. And BTWs, not that cute."

"As if I would be so shallow. Mum and dad like him."

"Another point in Wayne's favor."

"He is cuter."

"Right!"

"I mean, it's a low bar." They giggled some more. Some guy yelled at them from a few rows down, "Shard the fargub!" Another added charmingly, "Shaaz ya wooza!" A well-aimed Jaffa put a stop to that; but anyway, they settled in for a few minutes to watch the film. The heroine had been captured and bound in the villain's lair. All was lost—or so it seemed. But wait! It was a ruse all along! She had manipulated them so as to be trapped and forgotten in the corner where she could listen in on their dark plots.

"But with Wayne, it's just, I never know what he's about," said Sharon. "He's like, 'Hi, I'm Wayne Hope, I'm not like the other guys.' But I don't know if there's a lot of *there* there, ya know?"

"Yeah, nah, it's like, he's all Mr. Virtue one day, but when anything gets real, does he come through? He just seems kinda ... *blah*. Real 'Nice Guy' energy."

"Like, I don't want to make too big a deal of it. I mean, everyone does it. But it is my first time, so."

"God, you innocent virgin," laughed Mags, loud enough for a couple of rows to hear.

"Shut it, or I swear ..."

"Yeah? You swear what, exactly?"

Sharon tipped the bag of Jaffas over Mags and they both collapsed in hysterics. Meanwhile, the heroine escaped from her bonds and wreaked bloody vengeance on her captors. But it was bittersweet, for her beloved had arrived in a doomed attempt to save her, only to be ambushed by the villain, who escaped leaving the beloved dying in his heroine's arms. The poignancy of the moment was sadly lost on the two girls.

"Well," said Mags when they had recovered, "you're eighteen. It's your choice."

"Too bloody right it is."

"And you'll have to live with it."

The sequel had been set up and the credits were rolling. They got up, rather reluctantly, and filed out to the foyer. They knew it wouldn't be pleasant outside.

But things had gotten worse. Way worse. The fires were coming in fast. The sky was red and ashes blew horizontal. They looked out the window of the cinema, unsure what to do. The kids from the movie slowly gathered. As they watched, the mid-afternoon sun—that fierce unstoppable Australian sun—went dark and vanished altogether. The red turned to black. The ashes were now glowing embers, swirling in the gloom. Without warning there was a crack; something had exploded. The kids looked at each other nervously and the sisters held hands. Then another crack, and then, right in front of them, lightning smashed down on a telephone pole. They leapt back, suddenly terrified. There was a roar, like a sucking sound. It stopped for a second. Then of a sudden, fire surged above the buildings. Like a wall of liquid nightmares, all black and blazing, it ripped through the town, levelling buildings, tossing cars in the air, annihilating everything before it.

They watched in frozen horror, unbelieving. Then the window smashed and the fire came for them. Screaming they ran. Some of them made it back inside. Sharon was crying and shaking, clinging to her sister's hand. Then she turned and saw: it wasn't her sister. She'd grabbed some other girl's hand in the rush.

"Mags," she yelled. "Mags!" The doors to the cinema were shut, and no-one else was getting in. "Mags!" She pushed through the crowd, searching. She couldn't find her.

The cinema was solid and somehow it survived. But when they emerged an hour or so later, the rest of the town was gone. There was nothing there, just smoking wreckage. Mags was gone, all the kids outside were gone. They never found the bodies; there's not much left from a thousand degree firestorm.

After the roar and the chaos, a peace had settled over the place; the peace of nothing left to lose. The kids stepped out front of the cinema. The air was breathable, so long as they used their masks. And light was returning, still red, but enough to see.

It happened so fast. She knew it was going to be a hot day; when it cracks fifty, it's never pleasant. It's not like they hadn't seen that before. When she left her house, though, she thought she'd spend a couple hours in the cool. She just wanted to have some fun. She never thought. The fire took everything: her house, her sister, her family, her friends, her town. Even the stupid mice. All in a few minutes of chaotic inferno.

One of the kids checked the news on their phone and put it on speaker for them. "This just in, a message from the office of the Prime Minister, Cole Evermore. Given the extreme conditions over much of Australia, the election scheduled for tomorrow is cancelled. The Government regrets that with the disbanding of emergency services, it is not in a position to provide aid for citizens affected by unpredictable weather patterns. The Prime Minister has expressed confidence that the situation will soon return to normal, and reiterated his position that the Government cannot be held accountable for unforeseen events. His hopes and prayers are with you in your difficult times. In the meantime, however, he is happy to report that he has reached an unprecedented bipartisan agreement with the leader of the opposition, Wayne Hope. Given the extraordinary conditions, both leaders have announced that it is in the best interests of the people that the Constitution is suspended. As of now, Australia is under martial law."

"So I suppose I don't get to choose after all," said Sharon, to nobody in particular.

the far side of the sky (4)

Edgar pounded on the door. "It's me, Arixys, it's me! Open up, let me in."

Arixys woke with a jump; it was the middle of the night! They could hear the pounding and their father's voice. It took them a minute to realize that they weren't dreaming. They leapt up and ran downstairs; but just as they got to the door, they hesitated. They could see some other shapes through the glass, dark forms in the night. It wasn't just dad. Anyway, they pulled back the big bolt in the door and opened it with a smile.

Edgar was there, in the white that he always wore. But the big men in black with him had a bag; they pulled it over their head and grabbed them tight.

"No, stop!" screamed Arixys. "Stop! Dad!"

"Hush child, don't worry, it'll be over in a minute."

They hustled Arixys into a van, slammed the door and sped off. Edgar remained behind; he needed to finalize some things in their home.

Arixys was terrified, alone and bound in a car with strange silent men, abducted without warning with the aid of their father. Why had he done this? What was happening to them? They tried to breathe, but could only gasp under the hood. There were no answers, only fear, as the dark car vanished into the dark night.

language

"But sweetie, shouldn't they come through the *front* door? They're illegals, not refugees." said Katy's mum.

"Urrgh," said Katy. The Tesla was whipping down the freeway, just eating up those miles. The terrain was broad and flat: scrub, light industry, waste. Her mother was driving her home from band practice.

It was something she'd been doing for a while now. A couple of years ago Spencer, her friend from next door, came running into her room, saying, "Check this out!"

"What?"

"These guys, they're looking for a bass player."

"But I don't play bass."

"So what? They'll love you, you're amazing."

"I don't think that's how it really works ..."

"Anyway, the audition's booked. As your agent, I made an executive call."

"So ... you're my agent now?"

"For all they know."

It was kinda intimidating; a professional band of seasoned rock musos. Outside the rehearsal studio Spencer noticed Katy's nerves and took her hand, "Slay 'em babe. They're only boys." Katy squeezed her hand, took a deep breath, and went in.

The band was already hanging around, making some noise. Katy said, "I'm here from the ad? To audition?"

"No worries," they said, "Great, we need a bass player. If you've got the chops."

Katy grinned, "Sure, cool, get a cute chick on bass, right? Piss off, I'm playing lead."

The guys smirked as she plugged in, while Spencer sat back in anticipation; she knew what was coming.

Katy said, "So, what shall I start with? Some classics? Bieber?"

They said, "Whatever, just show us what you got."

Katy said, "Alright, well, I know *Smoke on the Water*, how 'bout that?"

The guys snickered, "Sure!! Blow us away." It was a notoriously basic beginner's riff.

Katy took her time fussing and getting the settings right, scratching out a couple of dodgy notes. "Here goes," she said, "Wish me luck, guys!"

She started. But it was no plodding dinosaur riff: she launched right into AC/DC's *Thunderstruck*. Her right fist punched the air as she hammered out the brutal, cascading arpeggios at lightning speed with her left hand. Spencer jumped up, laughing and head-banging with her friend, while the guys sat open-mouthed.

She stopped and said, "Oops, did I get the wrong song? Silly me!"

The guys said, "Holy crap, you've got the job. That was metal."

She fluttered her eyes innocently and said, "You don't need me to do the solo?"

So that was fun.

Anyway, today they had to cancel; no power. And here she was trapped in a car listening to her mum complain about asylum seekers. She had to say something. "You know mum, they say the brain operates in eleven dimensions."

"Really, sweetie? Wow!"

"I know right!" said Katy. "And I hope that they're right, because three dimensions are just not enough for me to roll my eyes in right now."

"Well, I was only saying."

"Seriously. These are human beings. Their homes have turned to shit ..."

"Language!"

"Sorry! Their homes have turned to *fuck* because of us, like literally our lifestyle has destroyed everything they have, and you, a product of that privilege, think it's okay to dehumanize them because the government decided to call them 'illegals'? Like, the problem is *insufficiently precise use of moral language*? I just fucking can't with this shit."

Katy turned to the window, and took out her phone to scroll some vids. Cute ... cringe ... lol ... oh god, not this conspiracy crap again. People were such idiots.

"I'm your mother, Katy. You will show a little respect."

"Are you though?" mumbled Katy. And more loudly, "Then I'm your daughter. Shouldn't you have left me a world I can live in?"

"Oh, teens, you're always so dramatic!"

Katy couldn't help herself. "*I'm* dramatic? See that fricking huge bushfire over there burning like the bowels of hell? Now that is a level of drama I can respect. You say you do everything for me. But did you ever think whether I want the things you have to give? I don't. I don't want a big house, a shiny car, I don't care about degrees or careers. I don't want none of this. Look around you, mum! That's actual smoke. Is this normal now? None of those things matter—everything is burning! What I want is air to breathe, ground to walk on, water to drink. Can you give me those things, mum?"

"Things are changing. Young people really care about the environment. I guess we can't have been *all* bad as parents!"

"And that's supposed to make it *better*?" Katy was seething now. "You set the whole world literally on fire, throw your kids in it, then congratulate yourself when we try to put it out? Why in the name of everloving fuck should I listen to anything you say? Cunt."

"*Katy!*"

"I'm sorry, that was an abuse of language. Cunts give life, so." That was super mean, and Katy knew it. She was adopted, obviously, and her mum, unable to have her own kids, had done her best to raise someone else's.

Katy was a firestarter, no doubt. But that's not all: she was a precocious student, a talented athlete, and in her down time, an enthusiastic advocate of equal-opportunity casual sex. But it was all getting too much. Something inside her was breaking.

It started when Spencer left. They'd grown up together. They shared everything. They played together, swapped clothes, laughed at boys. But one day, it was like there was a different person where her best friend used to be.

———————————————

You never got used to it. You couldn't turn around without some other disaster, some new and weirdly unexpected sign that the planet was done with us. Birds fell out of the sky. Fishing boats hauled only jellyfish. The tundra exploded with huge burps

42

of methane. People died in wet-bulb temperatures. Just the other week, it was so hot, a hundred thousand bats here in Sydney dropped dead right out of the trees. On the other side of the continent, Perth was in its dying days: there was nothing to drink, the wheat belt was dust, and the city was on the verge of collapse. Everywhere, people were struck with their own local version of what the media had taken to calling "escalating global chaos".

Scared and desperate, hot and angry, people turned violent. Insurrections rocked cities the world over, while governments struggled to maintain even basic operations. The worse the riots got, the quicker the cities fell apart. Much of the world had never really known what it was like to have a functioning government, and the rest of the world was rapidly finding out.

People were fleeing their homes in the hundreds of millions. Maybe billions, who was counting? The ones on the coast headed inland, the ones inland headed to the coast. They'd do anything to get away, but everywhere they went was more of the same. In Australia, extreme heat made the outback unlivable. Even Aboriginal people used to desert living couldn't escape the laws of physics. They were abandoning their lands and moving to cities, but the cities didn't want them.

Then there were the asylum seekers. They boarded any creaky old vessel they could find and set out for anywhere they could. They came from the deltas of the Mekong, the Ganges, and the Irrawaddy; from the sunken islands of the Pacific; from fishless shores swept with storms; from drowning cities built too close to the sea—Bangkok, Jakarta, Yangon, Colombo, Singapore, Dhaka, Phnom Penh, Chennai, Manila, Kuala Lumpur.

Once upon a time, politicians whipped up a panic over "boat people". "A nation needs borders!" they'd crow, basking in hate, as if a few desperate refugees were a dire threat to national security. People do so love a scapegoat.

But what to do when there are not thousands, but tens of thousands? Hundreds of thousands? Millions? There were plenty of nations around the globe that had already crumbled, abandoning even a semblance of central control and governance. At some point, the paranoid fantasies become reality.

At that point a nation faces a choice. What is more important: nationhood or humanity? Australians were not the kind of people who would slaughter unarmed innocents as a matter of state policy. At least, not without some hand-wringing first. Not everyone relished the idea of state-sponsored mass murder. But it proved easier to overlook once democracy had lapsed. Australia's government abandoned any treaties that bound it to humane treatment of the desperate and needy. And its people steeled themselves to do what had to be done. Or more to the point: they steeled themselves to tell their children to do what had to be done.

The grown-ups in charge sent out their blue-eyed sons and daughters to face the oncoming tide; in chopper carriers and nuclear submarines; in patrol boats, frigates, and destroyers; in squadrons of F-35s supported by Reaper drones.

Which is why it shook Katy to the core when Spencer told her she was joining the Navy. "I feel like I should serve," she said. It was her sixteenth birthday. It was hard to find recruits, so they had lowered the age limit.

"What the fuck, dude," said Katy with her usual tact. "When did you go all dark side?"

"Someone's got to keep us safe," said Spencer. "Not everyone's a pacifist like you."

"Yeah, well, I remember a few less than peaceful moments. But you know, 'I choose violence' is just a meme, right?"

"It's not about violence, it's about security."

"God, you sound just like one of them. You're gonna like, 'securely' shoot them? They'll be thrilled."

"It won't come to that. Show enough strength, they'll turn back."

"I seriously doubt that."

"Okay genius," said Spencer, "what's your solution? What do we do, actually? Just let them come?"

"Sure, of course. No-one owns the planet. Our home is their home. Everyone needs somewhere to live."

"So what, in your house? How many will you fit? You've got a couple of spare rooms. Heck, just sleep on the floor, give 'em your bed."

Katy didn't have an answer to that. "Look dude, just ... stay safe, okay? You know you're an idiot, and you'll probably get yourself killed?"

Spencer laughed, "No-one's getting killed, doofus. Don't worry, someone's got to do something, might as well be me."

Bootcamp was brutal, but Spencer did pretty well. She took every bit of crap they dished out, and through it all kept a steady hand and a clear eye. They trained her on the M242 Bushmaster autocannon. It was a no-nonsense bit of kit, a powerful and satisfying weapon

45

that was super fun to shoot. She liked the feel of it, the way you had to almost hug the weapon. It felt like part of you.

They started her out on a simulator that was as lifelike as possible. Over and over until it's second nature. It's them or us: breathe, aim, squeeze, fire. It's your duty: breathe, aim, squeeze, fire. You are the nation's protector: breathe, aim, squeeze, fire. Neutralize the enemy: breathe, aim, squeeze, fire.

But no simulation could ever match the real thing. The power, the force in it. When you squeezed the trigger, you felt all the kick, as the water erupted and the target shattered.

Her father was so proud of Spencer in her natty white uniform on the day of her graduation. It brought a tear to his eye to see his daughter marching smartly in rank at the naval academy. She was so young, yet she had accomplished so much!

Her first assignment was a "territorial integrity" mission on the destroyer HMAS *Sydney*. She kissed her father goodbye, gave Katy a hug, and set out across blue waters to face the incoming horde. As they drew near the boats, she grew nervous, and called to mind her training. Breathe, aim, squeeze, fire. What she had to do.

Over crackly tannoys, officers put on a polite but stern voice as they asked the people on the boats to turn around. They were professionals, and they stated their warning in language that was respectful, yet clear and unambiguous.

It was a day of dazzling sunshine. Spencer took a deep breath as she squinted into the sights on her Bushmaster, getting ready, all the while assuming they would turn back. She had no grudge against these people. But she did have her duty.

With the spectre of death snapping at their heels, the people in the boats had no incentive to stop. They sailed on into the teeth of the guns.

The officer issued another warning.

Spencer saw the boat clearly in her sights. The white sun was like an x-ray. She could see the planks, the crowd of dark-skinned people on board, the little children. She could see the white flags. And she could see that they weren't turning back. They were crossing an invisible line in the ocean. And she felt herself standing outside herself, watching events unfold with a sort of disturbed detachment. Like she saw herself squeeze the trigger and she knew what it meant but it was all happening too slowly. It couldn't be real. Reality wasn't in slow motion. This was such a cliché. Every wave, every glitter off the sea, was etched with epic significance. The people's emotions were too obvious, they were crying and huddling and waving white flags; it was all on the surface, where was the nuance? They seemed like actors badly playing terror. She remembered Katy, almost laughed inside at the memories of her life, or maybe it was never hers, it was all just pretend, like the people in the boat. Maybe she had been pretending her whole life. She knew she was losing her in that moment, her best friend, that moment as she was deciding, that moment right now, that moment she finally knew what kind of person she really was.

The officer called out, "Fire!"

She pulled the trigger. The boat in her sights disintegrated, erupting in a storm of splinters and white spray, just like her practice targets. It only took a few seconds.

She stopped, and could hear the sounds of other weapons targeting other boats. She scanned, found another, started firing. And again, and again.

Soon debris was floating past the massive steel bulk of their destroyer. She could see planks of wood, bits of superstructure, clothes, mangled bodies. There was a one guy, his arm off, but he was still alive, screaming and thrashing about in the shining sea.

All across the bright waters, a rain of hellfire was unleashed by sons and daughters, brothers and sisters, friends, colleagues, and lovers. Billions of dollars of military hardware finally found its true purpose: to annihilate leaky fishing boats full of people whose only crime was seeking a place to live.

The water was defiled with the blood of innocents and the desecrated corpses of skinny, brown-skinned children.

It was a policy success, they said. A demonstration of will. A testament to our investment in peace and security. But the boats kept coming. Soon they stopped asking before they fired. That's the kind of people we became. That's who we turned the children into. Hell, maybe that's who we were all along.

When Spencer came home on leave, Katy went to see her. She went to take her hand, but Spencer pulled it away. They sat there with nothing to say.

All this, and everyone just kept on going as if nothing had changed. It was just the smiles got tighter, the knuckles whiter, and everyone was more determined than ever to pretend it was all going to be fine.

It wasn't going to be fine. Fine was something old people said. Katy's generation didn't have the luxury of fine.

Her mum slowed, turned off the freeway. They were headed over the crossing-bridge, on a winding highway past shops and suburbs.

"You know, Katy, a mom always thinks ..."

"That their daughters will grow up nice and polite?"

"Well, yes. But that's not ... It's just, it used to be so much simpler. Girls were girls ..."

"Oh. *That.*"

"No, I mean, I understand that you're a lesbian."

"I'm bi mum. Thanks for knowing me."

"I know, honey. I guess ... I guess I thought that I'd be able to show you the world. That I had something for you. But you seem so ... so distant." She laughed, saying, "Oh but we're a pair, aren't we? I've become an old fogey, and you're something new." She paused, thoughtfully. "I just don't know if it's wise to throw out everything we had. It wasn't all bad, back then."

"I get it, mum, and I know: you love me, even though I say awful things. I know," said Katy. "But mum, *we didn't change it.* We're just trying to live in it."

"But that's just it! We didn't change it either! Or at least, we didn't mean to. No-one knew. It just ... happened."

Musing, Katy said, "I wonder."

"What?"

"What if it didn't? Just happen. What if it was deliberate."

"Who'd do it deliberately?"

"Well, maybe not consciously. I mean, does it matter? What if all the 'unintended' consequences were meant to happen?"

49

"I don't know …"

Katy was on a roll now. "Okay, what about racism. Does it just happen that people of color get the short stick, in education, in health, in justice? No, it's racism. Conscious or not, people want to hurt people with different-colored skin. So climate change comes along and surprise! The ones who suffer the most are poor, brown, and over there. Is it just coincidence? Does it just *happen* that the system works that way? Or was that the purpose of the system? Is that why it was built?"

"I guess … No, people want justice, it's just hard to do."

"It doesn't seem that hard. Treat people decently." Katy paused for a while, as the sweeping curves of the highway narrowed into suburban streets lined with old European trees. Her mum slowed down to take the corners gently; it was so up down and around, you'd easily get carsick if you didn't watch out.

"Oh god," Katy said. There was a sinking feeling in her gut. She'd just thought of something really horrible. She could almost feel the blood draining from her face.

"Katy, what? Are you okay?"

"What if that's what's happening in generations?"

"Sorry?"

"What if climate change is a punishment?"

"What? No!"

"Hear me out. Kids suck, right? I mean, look at me, look at how I talk to you. I'm sorry, I don't mean to, but I do it anyway. Don't you want to just, I dunno, give me a good strapping some times? Like they did in the old days?"

"No, sweetie. Well yes, you do test me. But I love you. You know that. I'd never hurt you."

"I do know that," said Katy. "But be honest: you totally would hurt me if it was a different time and place. If that was normal, you'd punish me for swearing at you. Isn't that what you religious people took from the Bible? 'Spare not the rod'? But now you're not allowed; it's not PC. What's that parents used to say as they were abusing their children? 'This hurts me more than it hurts you'? What if they were right? Where does it go? Where does the pain of the parents go? What if they just shove the pain underneath the love? What if love was part of the system? What if a mother's love for her daughter was what made it all possible?"

"I don't understand."

"Why do you love me, mum?" said Katy. "I smoke pot, I'm an atheist, I go to protests, I date girls. I've inked my body to make it mine, not yours. I'm everything you hate. And I treat you like crap. When was the last time I cleaned my room?"

"A mother doesn't need a reason."

"And there it is. It's irrational. It's divine. It's to be celebrated, not questioned. But what if there was a perfectly rational reason? What if mothers loved their kids *because* of all the terrible things we do?"

"Why on earth would love ..."

"Well, evolution for starters. Gotta keep the species going, right? All the pain, the danger, the burden that kids put on their parents, it's unbelievable. Jesus, what we put you through. We take twenty years of your life. The resentment, the loss: the love evolved to balance that, to stop it from getting out of hand. To stop you from hurting us too bad."

"Oh, sweetie, I don't know ..."

"But there's a contract. We become mini-yous. You pass on your values, your knowledge, your name, you continue in us. But we totally broke that deal. We could care less about your values, and your knowledge is useless. We've become all that you are not. We woke up. We've gone already, and you can't even see our path."

"No, Katy, no. That's not ..."

"So, climate collapse, huh? The olds make it happen, the kids suffer it. Our punishment. For being the brats that we are."

"No, oh god, no, Katy!" her mum started crying. "No!"

"What is my life, mum?" said Katy. She was tearing up, too. "How did everything get so lost?"

"I don't know," sobbed her mum. "I don't know." They had arrived home, pulled up at the driveway. They didn't wait for the car to stop before they pulled each other in, crying. They never did this. "I'm sorry, sweetie! I'm sorry I didn't do more. I'm so sorry." And they stayed that way as the sun set, hugging each other tight, crying on each other's shoulders.

"I love you so much," she said. And they didn't even know who said it any more.

Their house was on a steep incline; the other side was a gully of wild bush. The bush turkeys used to come up to their front lawn, while over the road was a palm tree with a dozen bin chickens come home to roost. At that hour, the sun cast its last rays through the leaves, dappling the house in red gold. It was getting deeper red these days, as the sky was tinged with fire and darkened with smoke.

But they could still hear the cicadas clacking and the frogs burping and the magpies tweeting. And from the ridge nearby a host of bats was waking, setting off in their evening swarm.

After a long while, they got out of the car. It was dark now. The lights in the house turned on and her mother looked up with hope. "We're home. Let's go in, I'll make us some dinner."

But Katy stood still. Everything dropped away. She wasn't in a narrow green street outside a comfy home with her mum, coming home from band practice. She was just ... nowhere. It wasn't dark or light, she wasn't in a time or a place. She was in-between.

She shook herself. Turning from her home and her mother, she said one word: "No." It was the only word she had left. She started walking.

"Katy, where are you going?"

She kept walking.

"Katy! Katy, what's up? Katy! *Katy!*"

Katy didn't turn around. Her mother's call winged out towards her, but faltered and fell along the way, like a starving bird crossing a too-wide desert.

She never went home. And she never saw her mother again.

As Katy's mum watched her vanish in the gloom, she rationalized it like she always did. "She just needs some time to herself. That was a lot, she has to process. She'll end up at Spencer's house, it's not like that hasn't happened before. She's sixteen, she can look after herself." Comforting words, words of hope. Words that made sense of a world that no longer made sense.

She went indoors, pushing aside the worry that gnawed inside her, and prepared dinner for two. She ate alone.

As the years passed, she diminished and faded to grey. She never got over the loss, but it would be a mistake to think that those final years were wasted. Before the end, she came to understand: it was she who had disappeared, while her daughter remained. She didn't blame her daughter, or herself for that matter. Katy was an angel and she had helped her find her wings. What could she do but fly away?

She never told anyone what her daughter had said to her. She never found the words.

the far side of the sky (5)

Dad,

How could you! What did you do! I am all alone in the big place. No-one will talk to me. I don't know what is happening. Help me! Take me home!

My dearest Arixys,

Hush, my child, be not afraid. I am sorry for how it unfolded, but we had to keep it all secret. You can trust the men, they will not hurt you. I will be with you soon, I promise. Just be patient a little while longer.

Arixys, you will not see your home again. Please be calm, let me explain what is happening. Breathe, remember? Breathe and be aware, you can always find your bliss within.

It is time, listen to me. I will tell you what is going on.

It was half a century ago, when the Americans and the Soviets started sending probes into space, that they made an incredible discovery. There is, in fact, a *second earth*!

When our solar system was formed, the scientists found, unimaginable forces spun apart in twin great spirals that solidified both as the planet we know as Earth, and as a second almost identical planet, exactly on the opposite side of the sun.

It was clear, even at the height of the Cold War, that this was something that transcended politics. Scientists the world over set to work to learn what they could about our mysterious twin. And what they found was beyond their wildest dreams.

Earth-2 is the same size as our Earth-1, occupying the same orbit around the sun. It has the same mix of land and oceans, and a varied but generally pleasant climate. And it is full of life! The land masses are vivid green, the oceans teeming with fish. The biology is carbon-based, almost identical with our own. Some speculate that an asteroid in the distant past seeded organic matter from one planet to the other. But the cause is secondary to the fact: Earth-2 is livable. It's better than livable—it's spectacular.

The first concern of our Leaders was to determine whether Earth-2 posed a threat. They scrutinized it for signs of intelligent life and found nothing. The highest form of life there is a species of rather adorable monkey-like creature.

Now, while the Leaders were learning all this, they were also learning about something else: anthropogenic global warming. By the early 1960s, the evidence was clearly pointing to the calamitous effects of our greed for fossil fuels. Politicians and scientists were moving towards a consensus that coal and oil must be rapidly phased out, and that we must transition to a fully renewable economy by the end of the 1970s.

But there was a concern. Some scientists were saying that we had passed certain tipping points and that the collapse of the environment was already locked in. We had cleared too many forests, burnt too much fuel, and scoured too much from the seas.

While this was uncertain, it raised a worrying problem. We could pour our effort into saving this world, and it might work—or it might not. We could introduce renewable energy and sustainable farming, and build energy-efficient houses. But there is just so much overhead. Too many cities are built for cars: how can they be made amenable for walking and public transport? How to reverse the long-standing trends of manufacturing, farming, transport, and a thousand other things, all built on the idea that we can just burn fossil fuels as much as we like? And how to do all this when every detail must be negotiated and agreed on by vested interests?

What if, some dared to wonder, we had the chance to move to a new home? Would it not be better to simply start again? Earth-2 appeared as a sign, a unique blessing. It would be a shame, folly really, to overlook such a chance. We have learned so much. Why not put it into practice and create a life truly worth living?

I must leave it there, for now. The story goes on, and the greater part is not yet revealed!

Stay strong, and rejoice, for our future is full of blessings!

Your devoted father,

Edgar

t-shirts

The order was not predetermined, but the start was always the same. He reached into the basket and pulled out a black t-shirt. On the front was a triangle, a prism, with a ray of white light and a rainbow. *The Dark Side of the Moon*, greatest album of all time. Then came the rest: *London Calling, Blonde on Blonde, Rumours, Sgt. Peppers, Born to Run, East*. One by one the icons of classic rock, damp, were carefully pinned to the line.

Chris stayed in place, moving the Hills Hoist around bit by bit. The yard was big enough, not huge by any means, but not one of those modern little boxes. The grass was brown, the house was fibro. For a gardener, his own garden was spartan.

He was pretty efficient. A couple of minutes later, they were all done and the hoist came around again. He unpinned the black t-shirt, bone dry already, and then the rest. One by one and the ritual was over. Some people still used clothes dryers, said it was more convenient. He was not one of those people. Not that he was a greenie or anything, he just didn't see the point when the clothes dried faster than you could pin them up.

Taking the basket he went back inside where it was just as hot. Not too bad, you could put the fan on. To be honest, mostly he sat around shirtless; the whole t-shirt thing was pretty much formal wear at this point.

Settling at his desk, he fired up Youtube. His feed was always informative: "What they aren't telling you about the plague!" "Climate change: hoax or coverup?" "How the elites invented the environment!" You know, that kind of stuff. He clicked play. At least it was some noise in his empty house.

He knew there had to be a reason he lost her. These things don't just happen. He needed to understand. What was going on? What hidden currents stole his love away? He drifted into his thoughts. Like a deep river he could see her. She was swimming, swept with the current, waving happily, her slender arm back and forth, smiling like a naiad as she vanished in the mist.

He was daydreaming again, he had to get over it. Shaking his head, he came to a decision. He couldn't just keep on like this, he had to do something. He shut off the clip. It was about how mind-controlled monkeys had stolen zombie anthrax, injected it into genetically-engineered mutant murder hornets, and traded them with aliens in exchange for actual real bananas. Which, to be honest, was a bridge too far even for him. Everyone knew bananas weren't a thing any more. He stepped outside, flinching; you never really get used to the searing burn of the sun.

At the back of his yard was an old tin shed. He used it for his gardening stuff. It was full of tools and chemicals, but lately it was neglected. What was a gardener to do when all the gardens were dead? Still, he opened the door and looked it over, thinking, "It's a start."

"I'll need an inventory," he said to himself. "A list. What's going to be useful, what is not. Steel buckets, yes, plastic buckets, no. Knives, spades, gloves, all yes. Herbicide, no. Pesticide ... nah, it'll be off in a few years anyway. Petrol, same. Nothing electric. Nothing with a motor. Kerosene lamp? How long does kerosene last? Okay, another list, things to check. Oil, yes. Rags, no, I'll be able to get them. Oh yeah, and seeds. Lots of seeds."

He worked until the sun went down, ignoring the streams of sweat, sorting out it all out: what is going to be useful when the world has ended? He was going to have to find a better place to keep it all, maybe a cave in the mountains. Somewhere with water. But at least it was something to do. At least it kept his hands and mind busy.

They took his love away, but damned if they were going to take his life.

the far side of the sky (6)

Dear Arixys,

I haven't heard from you in a while. I hope you're okay! It's taking longer than I thought, but I am nearly ready to join you. We will be together soon, I promise.

Let me continue the great story!

When all options had been carefully considered, the right course of action was clear. Our Leaders undertook humanity's greatest task: a multi-decade project preparing a world worthy to become humanity's new home. This finally explains why our politicians have seemed so unconcerned with climate catastrophe, so blasé that they allow our planet to career frantically towards collapse. This is where all the missing trillions have gone, not to tax havens for the ultra-rich. I mean really, who could possibly be so evil as to syphon funds from the public purse when the fate of humanity is at stake? The rich may have their flaws, but that would be truly monstrous!

No, the great and the good have been secretly laboring behind the scenes, building a paradise. It turns out, all our Leaders wanted was for us to live and flourish on a new world.

And what a world it is! Let me explain how it all works.

From the beginning, it was determined that the planet itself would be zoned residential. The value of the environment, after all, lies in how it serves humanity. If we shift industry off-planet, we can truly maximize the utility of the ecosphere.

Mining is carried out in the asteroid belt, where a complex network of robotic workers extract practically limitless quantities of any mineral. Solar and nuclear energy powers refining and manufacturing. Waste and pollution are a non-issue, as they are simply expelled to the infinity of space. Finished goods are sent to the "Celestial Amazon", a grand network of satellites that organizes distribution. Meanwhile, huge orbiting greenhouses grow abundant food of every variety. In this way the foods of Earth-1 can be enjoyed without contaminating the biosphere of Earth-2. Space elevators silently and swiftly convey goods to the surface. Solar-powered drones bring any kind of product right to your door, while garbage drones remove all waste harmlessly to space.

The smart part is, all these machines are self-replicating, self-repairing, and self-improving! When they break down, they fix themselves up, or another machine fixes them. When they need more energy or more materials, they mine what they need from the asteroids. They never rest, they don't go on strike, and they never have a sick day—they are the perfect workers! Any spare time is devoted to designing and building better machines, all dedicated to the good of humanity. There is nothing but infinite growth and infinite productivity, forever!

Much work has gone into construction. Promising sites are selected by teams of geologists, ecologists, botanists, and other specialists, who carefully survey the planet to determine the most beautiful and pleasant places to live. Architects have designed living spaces that harmonize with nature. Great tree-houses wind around 300-meter high forest giants. Houses on stilts have glass floors for watching mysterious forest beasts prowl below. Floating cities move between continents, allowing the citizens to enjoy the endless delights of the various climates. There is even a local plant with a giant flower, several meters across, large enough that cozy living spaces have been provided within the golden petals.

All of this, of course, took an unprecedented investment of money and resources, and in the meanwhile Earth-1 has sadly languished. Scorched by fire, drowned by flood, stripped of her mineral wealth, she lies broken and bleeding, spasming in the throes of a terminal decline. This is, of course, regrettable. Nobody wants to leave their mother in such a state. But it was a necessary sacrifice, and when you see the wonders of Earth-2, I'm sure you'll agree that it was worth it.

Okay, okay, I hear you! "When are we moving?" you cry! I cannot reveal the date, but rest assured, it will not be long.

Forgive me, I must finish here. I will be joining you very soon!

with love always,

Edgar

just the basic facts

"Mmm, pastries!"

"Ahh, may I say, yummsies!"

So it seemed the pastries were a hit, big surprise. It'd been a busy morning already: choose her outfit, do her hair, her makeup, an extra ten minutes to make it just so. Another ten minutes to double-check her presentation, then another ten to pick up the pastries on the way to work. Allow ten more for random incidents, and a final ten to negotiate the crowds in the square outside, always protesting something or other. Yesterday it was a ban on fossil fuels; today's mob wants what ... oh, their God-given right to keep driving gas-guzzling SUVs. Okay then.

Getting to work on time was a job of work.

Eager hands snatched up the pastries; they knew that if it was from Leslie, it was quality merch. Real hand-made pastries from a cute little shop nearby. They were gone in a flash. That made her happy.

"Well, I'm celebrating," said Leslie. "Yesterday we finalized the loan, so today we own our very own home!"

"Congrats!"

"Awesome!"

"Huh, one day I'll be as together as you, I swear!"

"Now we've got ya!" interjected her boss. "Ha ha!" There was an awkward pause. "Joke!"

"Sure," said Leslie. "It's just that ... my boyfriend's boss told him the same thing."

"Well, ain't that a thing?" enthused the boss. "Okay, so while we enjoy Leslie's *delicious* pastries—mm hmm!—how about we also enjoy her powerpoint?"

"Right," said Leslie. "Here goes ... wait a min ... oops there we are. Okay, so these are just preliminaries. But the figures show that over the last quarter we continued to experience significant growth in market share. That's 18% over our closest competitors, and 6% overall market share."

"Wow, okay!" said the boss. "A big round of applause for the team that made this happen!" And they clapped on cue.

"Ahh, yes, well," said Leslie. "But other metrics paint a different picture. While the size of the market continues to expand as expected, medium-term projections show a levelling off, followed by, well, decline and collapse, obviously."

"Best focus on the positive, right?" encouraged her boss. "I'll take the good news upstairs, they'll be so happy to hear it."

"Umm, okay," said Leslie. As a junior analyst, she focussed on assimilating the data and communicating it. She was great with details; policy wasn't her job. She knew that her boss would leave out most of the facts that she had so painstakingly gathered, and as usual, would also omit to note that she had done all the work. Still, it wasn't so bad; at least she had a job, a well-paying one at that.

Her firm, SmarticAIte, was a content farm. Their slogan was "Don't educate, SmarticAIte!" They created text, images, graphics, and video for a wide range of media, including social, advertising, student essays, news reports, novels, scripts, academic and scientific articles, legislation, legal judgments, school curricula, medical research, engineering assessments, intelligence gathering, and so on.

Clients gave them a brief, with style, media, size, and, optionally, some basic facts, and SmarticAIte did the rest. They called it an "AI-enhanced targeted content creation model".

What really happened was they fed the parameters through a neural net which created the artificially-generated content (AGC), then they gave the results to the clients. These days, no content provider could stay in business using human-generated content (HGC); you just couldn't write things fast enough.

SmarticAIte specialized in what corporate called "dynamic client interaction scenarios", where both sides of an adversarial system threw AGC at each other.

Competing news outlets, for example, bought different AGC reports on the same topics. Then they bought op-eds criticizing the takes of the other side. They were moving to an "pre-emptive interdependence" model where the attack pieces were created at the same time as the original report.

Academic work was no different. Professors skimmed the journals for some current topics and used that to seed their next article. Then some other professor would "write" a rebuttal. There were downsides to this, as progress in science and other intellectual fields had effectively halted. The AIs, by their nature, could only process what was past and rehash it for the present. Still, it didn't seem to matter too much, as most academic HGC was never read anyway.

Government departments used AI to frame legislation. The different parties would run it through AIs again to create revised versions to argue about. Once it had passed into law, lawyers would litigate the legislation with contrarian takes supplied by SmarticAIte. This had proven so successful that SmarticAIte was now rolling out an end-to-end legal solution. A suspect would be charged by AI, their case submitted to an AI court, their defence supplied by another AI, and an AI judge would give the verdict. It was fast, efficient, cheap, and reasonably accurate.

They'd make an AGC curriculum for the education department in a few minutes, which would become required for all students in the nation. But of course, the students would cheat in their tests—it was hardly regarded as cheating any more, just "artificially-optimized learning outcomes"—and give AGC answers back, which were then marked by, you guessed it, another AI. Arguably, there was little point in teaching students to write essays when no-one was going to read them anyway.

SmarticAIte handled sensitive private information such as medical and psychological records under a special, expensive, "crypto-AI" process. That didn't mean anything, actually, it was just bog-standard content processing. Occasionally the client would discover this and sue them. But it turns out that when you have AI lawyers on your side, it's cheaper to just pay the legal costs.

AGC was used by medical and welfare providers to improve efficiency in delivery outcomes. Abandoning the complex, error-prone, and inefficient legacy approach of measuring outcomes in terms of health and well-being, they moved to a sentiment-based approach where success was measured purely in terms of client satisfaction. When a client attempted to register their dissatisfaction, they would engage with an AI, which would swiftly generate content explaining why the client was mistaken in believing that they were dissatisfied and showing that the provider's failure to supply their basic services was in fact critical to the client's current state of satisfaction. As a result of these advanced logic parameters, client dissatisfaction was at a record low.

Of course, in reality anyone could simply make their own AGC, as these models were trivial to run. But SmarticAIte was founded on the one abiding principle of techno-supremacist capitalism: the more it cost, the more it was worth. They were proud to be the world's first tech company that employed no programmers at all. All their tech was created by, you guessed it, AI. The main thing the company actually did was to persuade their clients to pay for what they could have done themselves for free.

Still, it was an ethical company, so Leslie didn't feel too bad about her job. They had an equal-opportunity hiring policy, and targeted zero emissions. Their massive server farms were located in pods on the sea floor off New Caledonia, where they had little environmental impact as they simply re-used trenches devastated by deep-sea mining. True, they pumped a few billion kilojoules of heat into the warming oceans, but what was that in the scheme of things? In times past, those waters were spawning grounds for the same eels who made their home in the Parramatta river. But the eels were gone, so what was the harm in heating up the dead waters?

Meanwhile, the offices were provided with saunas, exercise and meditation rooms, a variety of five-star cuisine options, even an in-house escort service for lonely employees. And if their product was just rehashed "content", people didn't mind all that much. The world's intellectual activity had been reduced to recursive neural networks parroting each other. Yet somehow it didn't seem like such a big deal in the scheme of things, what with everything else that was going on.

SmarticAIte sold all of this content from their shiny HQ in downtown Parramatta. They had taken over a fifty-five story tower, in a move praised by the local MP as marking "a vital step forward into a new age of betterment together". His speech was, of course, written by SmarticAIte. Leslie worked with the staff on the fifty-forth floor, while the bosses were on the fifty-fifth. The rest of the building was kept deliberately empty; the long elevator ride made an impression on clients.

In a way, working for an AI company was one of the few reliable jobs left. Everyone else was at risk of being replaced by AI. But the AI companies knew how AI worked, and they'd never rely on it for themselves; it was strictly for the clients. She did the company reports the old-fashioned way: gathering facts, entering them, and writing up the results. She knew her value; her reports were good.

She focussed on getting the job done. One task, then the next. Don't look too far ahead. Do what was in her power. She had a good job, a good life. It should be enough.

"Hey gorgeous!" said a voice behind her and she pretended to be surprised.

"Dan!" Of course, the cameras had ID'd him when he got in the elevator, and he had to pass security, but they had this little thing where they kept some spontaneity. He was old-school. "How's it hanging, loser?"

"You know, missing my sweet girl," he laughed.

"Since this morning?"

"You were gone so fast!"

"I know, another report."

"And you're busy now, I'm guessing."

"It's as if you know me," said Leslie. Dan always popped by just to say hi and give her a kiss, he was really thoughtful. But today, she had a surprise for him. "Here babe, I got these, there's still one for you! Hand made and everything."

"Wow, that looks delicious, thanks."

"And can I ask a favor? Would you pick up a box of tampons, my period came early?"

"Of course, babe. You want me to bring them here?"

"No, I'm good for now. Tonight's fine."

They kissed and he sauntered out, chomping on the éclair and leaving her with a smile.

At five, she cleared her desk and made her way to the elevator. She noticed one of her colleagues coughing, a sound that always triggered a certain level of anxiety.

"You okay?" she asked, with genuine concern.

"Sure, yeah, just a, you know, catch in the throat. It's nothing."

"Alright, well, stay good. See you tomorrow!"

"No worries!"

Another colleague sniffed, a little shiftily. Nothing'd get you fired quicker than a disease. Hoping things would be okay, she took the elevator down and drove home. In her bag was the one remaining pastry, a custard pie; this was for her.

Dan hadn't got home. Concerned, she tried to ping him, but there was no response. A couple hours later, she got a notification from the hospital. They said he'd been admitted; he was in quarantine. Now she was scared. But they said it was just for observation.

There were no visitors till tomorrow. So she ate the custard pie and watched some (AI-generated) comedy to lift her spirits. If she couldn't sleep, well, there were always some pills.

The next day, still no news. But she couldn't worry too much, she had another report to give before visiting the hospital. She rushed in to work, pushed through the protestors outside, and rode up to the top.

The office was empty. It was so weird. She did a double-take—was it a holiday? Nope. This never happened, people were always on time. Then the first notice came from a colleague: "cant make it sorry, coughing this morning." Then another: "took a turn last night, I won't be coming in." And another and another.

Everyone, it seems, was out sick. Everyone except her; she must have been immune or something. Worried, she checked the feeds. They all spoke of a new plague, faster and deadlier than the others. It had apparently leaked from a local lab. It turns out it was a SmarticAIte subsidiary that was doing AI-based genetic experimentation, looking for a vaccine for the last plague. But this new one got into the food chain. Anyone handling food could transmit it. Several outlets in Parramatta had been identified as vectors.

With a cold chill, she realized, "It was the pastries. Oh my god! It was in the pastries!" She frantically began calling, trying to find her boyfriend, her friends, her boss. There was nothing. No-one was answering. Grabbing her things, she fled the empty office and headed for the hospital. But it was all on lockdown, armed guards outside. There were no visitors or voluntary admissions, just rendition at the front and trolleys hauling bags out the back.

She tried to explain that she was immune, that her boyfriend was inside. The guards wouldn't listen. When she tried to push her way in, they smashed her face with a rifle-butt, kicked her down the stairs, and maced her for good measure.

Bleeding, she staggered away from the hospital and the guards, trying to find safety.

When she got to her car, it wouldn't open.

"Face not recognized!" it said cheerily.

"Yeah, it just got mangled by a goon with a gun. Let me in, you artificial idiot."

"Face not recognized!"

She tried wiping her face down, cleaning up, but it wouldn't let her in. It was too much. She'd grab a ride home and try to figure things out. She pulled out her phone, "Ahh, get me a ride from here back home."

The app's AI responded, "Credit not accepted."

"What?" she said. "Use my SmarticAIte card. It covers everything."

"I'm sorry," the app responded, "SmarticAIte is no longer recognized."

"The hell!" She hadn't checked her phone in a minute, but there it was. Implicated in the latest plague, not even SmarticAIte's artificial lawyers could protect them. The company was bankrupt and the founders had skipped the country as wanted men.

"It's only 9:30," spat Leslie as she started to walk home. "Great, what next?" It was an hour in the increasingly hot sun, with her bruises and sprains not making things any easier. Finally though, she made it home and felt a small measure of relief as she limped up to her front door, really hers since yesterday. A place of her own.

But the door wouldn't unlock. Normally it'd do gait recognition when she came near. But she was tired and limping, maybe that was it. She tried to unlock the house screen with her face. That too didn't work; which was not unusual for people like her. Iris recognition: nope, her eyes were red and puffy from the mace. She tried her finger on the screen, but it was too messed up with sweat and blood. No-one used PINs any more, IDs were all based on bodies. Which was fine until they broke the bodies. She was so frustrated, she tried a few more times without thinking.

Then came the dread message: "Too many access attempts detected. Break-in suspected. Legal analysis pending ... pending ... pending. Congratulations! We have reached a verdict in your case. You have been charged, tried, and convicted of attempted breaking and entering. Guilt probability: 97.76%. Sentence: five years in prison for crimes against private property. Judicial services proudly brought to you by AdjudicAIte, the smart court that's fair and balanced. Your legal defence was proudly supplied by AttornicAIte, the smart lawyer in *your* corner. Please stay where you are. Law enforcement officers will shortly be with you to facilitate your transition to federal custody. This service proudly brought to you by SmarticAIte: smart solutions for stupid problems. Don't forget to like and subscribe. And remember: as the world gets dumber, SmarticAIte just gets smarter!"

She stared at the screen. No, this wasn't possible. The company didn't even exist any more! How could it be putting her in jail? The programs must be just running on autopilot; there's no-one to turn them off. Nothing left but the ghost AI in the machine. Then in the distance, the sirens. Oh crap.

Spinning, she fled her own home, dodging down the street and out of sight.

All her life, she had worked harder than everyone else, better than everyone else. She'd come from nothing, done all the right things. Doors had been slow to open and fast to shut. She had kept going and had built a life, a good life, for herself.

But she was no fool. She knew what mattered at the end of the day. She had been kind, giving, intelligent, dedicated, loyal, reliable. But what she did and who she was inside, that was meaningless. It was what she was on the outside that defined her in the eyes of others. And if she didn't act fast, right now, she wouldn't make it till nightfall. Not with the panic out there and the cops after her.

She ducked down an alleyway, behind some wheelie-bins. She knew what she had to do.

For starters, ditch her phone, they'd use it to track her. And her watch. Jewelry, it had ID chips in it. Shoes, jacket, piercings, same.

She kept on down the alley until she saw some bags of rubbish; a neighborhood like this, they were always tossing good stuff. Ripping open some bags, she found clothes. She stripped and started putting them on.

"Oh shit, my tampon," she realized. That'd have "health" tracking in it, for sure. They never lose a chance to creep on a girl. "Great timing, moon goddess!" Squatting in an alley, pulling out her tampon: she really hoped no-one was watching. She threw it in the rubbish. "I guess I'll just bleed like nature intended. Oh wait, no, they'll track my blood. Terrific. They can probably smell it." Rummaging, she found some used chux. "That'll have to do."

74

Next, she needed to scrub the makeup off; even that had nano-chips in it. All she had was dirt, so she grabbed a handful and rubbed it all over her face, scraping off all she could.

She found an old lighter in the rubbish. Good, she lit the whole lot. Pulling on some sneakers she bolted, leaving the rubbish of her life to burn.

"Oh, that's just fantastic," she thought, feeling her neck as she ran. That had a tracker in it too. Oh crap, and her tooth, she'd got a false tooth last year. Well, they had to go.

There was a burned-out old car wreck on some abandoned lot. She pulled open the boot, found the toolkit: a Stanley knife and some greasy pliers. This was not going to be pretty.

Okay, so, pliers. She'd just have to yeet the little bugger right out. Hard as you can, on the tooth, then yank! Ow, still there. Okay, again. Harder. Still nothing. She couldn't waste time. So: back and forth, she leveraged it, loosening it, then another rip. Finally it came out, with a spurt of blood. That really hurt.

Right, next, knife. She thought the implant was on the right side of the neck, but she couldn't feel anything. Well, here's hoping. She spat on the knife, cleaning it as best she could. It wasn't the sharpest. She put it against her neck, breathed deep, then cut. It didn't go in, she had to saw it. Okay, now we're in. She had to go deep enough to find the chip, but not so much as to sever an artery or whatever. She felt it, the tip seemed like it nicked something hard. A stroke of luck. She probed, angled, pulled, until it came; just a tiny speck of silicon.

Great, now … looking around, she saw what she needed: a rock. She put her tooth and the chip on a brick, and smashed them hard as she could, and again and again. Pounding away she thought,

"From AI to rocks in a morning. Now that's progress!" She cackled hysterically, imagining what she looked like, covered in blood and dirt, frantic and exposed.

When the chips were reduced to dust, she took off again. She knew the next hour or so was critical. If they found her, she was finished. But if she got past that, they'd have the next thing, and they'd be moving on. Then she could maybe start thinking about putting her life back together. After all, she wasn't actually guilty of anything except wearing her own skin.

She ran past the backs of houses, the unconscious of suburbia. Fences falling down, graffiti, vines overgrowing. Then she saw it: an abandoned construction site. She stopped, panting. There were big piles of loose yellow sand. She knew how to hide. She needed two things. There, behind that house, more castoffs. She pulled it apart, found what she needed, a pair of stockings. One more thing ... there, a hose, a few metres, good enough.

Back at the building site, she lay at the bottom of the sand pile, and started dragging it down over her legs, her torso. Then she pulled the stocking over her head, leaving only her mouth for the hose. She covered herself up completely, just the end of the hose left out for breathing.

She lay deathly still. Her heart was pounding, her breath was heaving, but she just focussed and stilled them both. It was dark and cool. Breathing was not easy, but when she settled, she didn't need much air.

Strangely, it was not the events of the morning that pressed upon her as she lay silent under the earth. It was the earth itself, its coolness and dryness, its steady weight. Somehow she felt calm. Like she had become a still point.

She even heard them, the cops, coming down the alley. They'd follow her here, she knew they would, up to where she destroyed the chips. She knew the sound of their feet. But she wasn't scared. She felt safe, somehow. Like so long as she didn't move, nothing could touch her. Like, she suddenly thought, a hunted animal.

The cops didn't stay long. Yes, they might have noticed the freshly disturbed earth on the building site. But it wasn't exactly Sherlock Holmes we were dealing with here. They walked past, grunted a bit, then wandered off.

Even after they left, she stayed. There was no hurry. After a good long while, she pulled herself out and shook off the sand.

She knew her next job, if she was to ever stand a chance. She had to look respectable again. Clothes, hair, shoes. Without them, she was just more street trash. Without them, people would see her for what she really was.

the far side of the sky (7)

Dad, you bastard. I hate you. Go away and die.

Dear Arixys,

Please don't be angry with me! It pierces me to the heart! I am on my way, and will arrive a few days after you get this letter. Please understand the secrecy, the danger we are all in if this gets out! Not everyone will understand! That's why we cannot use any electronic communication, only hand-delivered letters. But anyway, I like it, it gives me a sense of connection with you to know that your hands will hold these pages.

The future is almost upon us! Soon, we will join the steady stream of settlers. The Chosen, we are called. We will board an advanced spacecraft, soar up beyond the heavens, coast gently for a few weeks in space, then arrive at our new home. I, as a recognized Enlightened Master, have the honor of being called to the Chosen as spiritual adviser, and you will come as my heir.

Not everyone will be so fortunate, of course; we cannot get all eight billion humans transported in time. Unfortunately, some will have to be left behind. Still, roughly a million people will be resettled, more than enough to ensure the robust viability of the species.

That leaves us with a dilemma: who is to stay and who is to go? This is one of the hardest choices our Leaders faced, yet they did so with their usual far-sighted wisdom and selfless compassion. They are evolved beings. And they understand that among the peoples of this earth, there is a hierarchy of moral value. This is surely self-evident to any thinking person. Consider those who endorse racism, or who believe that women should be treated as less than equal, or whose minds are full of hate and greed. Clearly, they are just as human as we, but they are a lesser—I don't want to say "breed", but perhaps a lesser state of evolution.

It is, after all, because of *them* that we are in this pickle. *We* have always known that true happiness comes from spiritual things, not from the material. *We* didn't chop down forests or slaughter animals or beat women or hate gays. (Note: Unfortunately, no homosexuals are allowed among the Chosen. This is due to our overriding genetic imperative to continue the species, and is *not* homophobic.) We tried to do the right thing. We arranged executive mindfulness retreats and paid a premium for organic vegetables. We were not perfect, to be sure, but at least we tried.

Since the selection is based on spiritual evolution, I was delighted to find that meditators feature strongly among the Chosen. Indeed, among the group of Chosen to whom I was privileged to be invited, most looked like they were plucked straight from the front cover of a yoga magazine.

Not so fortunate are traditional religious followers, who just do rituals and make merit and worship images with flowers. They will stay behind. Not to speak of the followers of, shall we say, certain other religions, whose unenlightened views condemn them to a backwards morality of hate and division. Sad to say, there are many who, through no fault of their own, have not had the benefit of the cultural and educational uplift that would allow them to participate fully in an enlightened society. It is truly unfortunate, and while the

Leaders have striven to be as inclusive as possible, at the end of the day, a choice must be made.

Other criteria are also relevant for the choosing. The Chosen should be young, and since they are to be the future of humanity, nubile. Mostly teenage girls, in fact. Which is a nice balance, given that—through what is, I am sure, a purely non-sexist historical accident—the Leaders are all older men. They are men of letters, captains of industry, titans of intellect, serious fellows committed to innovation and progress. Though somewhat advanced in age, they will find no rest in the new world, for they will take on the essential duty of pairing up with multiple partners to ensure the propagation of our species. Oh, to think that future generations will be blessed with such genetic bounty!

All of these great secrets have been revealed to me only slowly, as they have been to you, Arixys. We are all in this together! I recall the first time I met my fellow travelers, and looked around me at the faces of the Chosen. Some of them you would recognize; but I am bound by deep oath to reveal no names. It is an inspiring and uplifting experience to be surrounded by so many noble men and women, whose serene beauty radiates a true sense of mankind's highest potential. A pure and elevated race, humanity shining at its most fair and golden!

It is, finally, with a sense of sad yet inevitable resignation that I contemplate the fate of the souls left behind. I derive no joy from the thought of the dark and unwashed masses scurrying like rats from the flooding shores of poisoned water, to find only slaughter at the hands of rabid mobs fleeing the dust and drought of the interior. Indeed, I feel boundless compassion and loving-kindness when I think of the poor children, diseased and starving in the ashes of the world we ruined, cowering in pain and despair as the scorching sky spits hot acid onto blistering soil.

Never will they be forgotten.

So long as lifeless seas lap upon lifeless shores, the brothers and sisters we left behind will remain in our prayers and meditations. We shall radiate them with pure, selfless love from our wondrous home on the far side of the sky.

Yours in exaltation,

Edgar

the town hall

"It's all about the skillz," said Katy. "You gotta know when, where, and how. And most of all, who."

"Who?" said Sharon.

"Yeah, like who's going to give you a second glance."

"You mean, find the person with the most humanity, and just exploit that?"

"Not the most humanity, the most money. And guilt."

They sat near the steps of the Parramatta Town Hall. It was a hot day, but early morning it was still livable. People were coming and going, getting to work, chatting on their phones. Some sat in the yard out front of St Johns. Shops were opening up, some of them anyway. Sheltered somewhat in a doorway, the girls contemplated their opportunities.

"Okay, so see that guy?" said Katy. "The suit on his phone?"

"Yes."

"Too busy, too preoccupied. It's a coping strategy."

"What do you mean?"

"I mean, no-one's really that busy, come on. To have so many desperately urgent things that you can't walk for five minutes without making a deal? Yeah, right. That guy's a douche who thinks he's a bigshot."

"Okay, but what do you mean, coping?"

"Well, so here we are, two homeless girls, sitting here all vulnerable and shit. What a guilt trip!"

"Seriously? You think he feels guilty?"

"No, exactly, that's my point. He's found a coping mechanism: stay busy, stay focused, don't notice. The trick is, everyone actually is human. They feel guilt, they feel shame. That's our in. We just have to find them as are not dealing with it."

"Hmm, okay," said Sharon. "What about him?"

"Maybe," said Katy, looking over the older, tired-looking gentleman shambling across the square. "The shirt's well-worn, but a good cut on it. And he's got that, I guess, sense of dignity to him? He's what, Chinese? Vietnamese? He has some culture, some values. He's carrying himself like he knows who he is." Decisive, she stood and walked over to the gentleman in question.

"Excuse me sir," she said. "My friend and I, we're sleeping rough. I don't want to bother you, but would you spare us a little? We haven't eaten today."

"Oh, I'm sorry, young lady!" he said, genuine concern on his face. "Here, have a twenty. Get yourself something to eat."

"Thank you kindly, sir," said Katy.

"And that," she said to Sharon when she got back, "is how it's done. It's all about maximizing return on investment."

"Twenty bucks, that'll get us what? Half a sandwich?"

"Pretty much. It's not nothing."

A dog wandered by, stubbornly ignoring their need to pat him. Katy leaned back against the wall, while Sharon kept checking for likely marks. Across the square walked a young woman, a few years older than them—mid-20s? Sharon nudged Katy and they watched as she came closer.

"Do I recognize her?" said Sharon.

"There's something," said Katy. "I wonder."

The young lady had on a tidy grey business getup. Pretty yet sensible shoes. She looked like she was heading for the office. But the white shirt was a little crumpled. And she carried a bag, like a sports bag, not something for the office. She walked uncertainly, nervous, glancing down.

"Hey," said Sharon. "What's up?" This was against protocol: you never treated marks as equals, you always had to approach them as less-than. But Sharon saw something in her.

The third woman hesitated, checking them over in turn. Making up her mind, she came over and said, "Hi, I'm Leslie."

"Sharon."

"Katy."

"You girls, ahh, sleeping rough?"

"For today, looks like," said Katy.

"I'm so sorry, I don't know what to do. I lost my home yesterday. I've got nowhere to go." It seemed this was the first time she'd said it, maybe the first time she'd really known it. She looked super vulnerable in that moment, the tears were close to the surface.

"So sorry, babe. Come on, sit down." Katy jumped up and gave her a hug.

The new girl sat on the steps. Katy noticed how she put the bag down on her far side. Smart. "God, how did I get here," she said. "I had a job, a career, a mortgage. A boyfriend! Then the company crashed, and it all just ... went away. I can't believe I thought it was something solid."

"And the guy?" said Katy.

"Yeah nah, a virus got him. Or I gave it to him, I think. He's still alive, maybe, but who knows where? He can't have long. Once they

84

take you for cleaning, well, you ever heard of anyone coming back?" It was a rhetorical question.

They sat there for a while, until Leslie asked, "If you don't mind, how did you get here?"

"Fire," said Sharon.

"Ahh, suburban ennui?" said Katy. "There didn't seem much of a life there."

"And that's just like, it? You just ended up here?"

"Well no," said Sharon. "When the fire took my family and my town, I tried to find somewhere. A family took me in for a while. Then it got too much, they were falling apart themselves. I ended up in the city, couch-surfing. It was pretty messed up. There's not a lot of places you can feel safe. Anyway, the last place I was at, there was a guy on some sort of pills, he tried to rape me."

"Oh my god," said Leslie.

"Yeah well, it happens. He thought I owed him something. Not sure why, 'cos he was a bloke? But not this time, I bit his balls off."

"This, this right here?" said Katy as Leslie gasped. "Legendary! Champion! It's like some god-tier king shit."

"Well, it felt like the thing to do at the time. I didn't really think it through, the blood was a lot, and the giblets. And the screaming. But yeah, they really didn't want me staying after that. Then I ran into this reprobate, who encouraged all my worst tendencies."

"Love you too," said Katy.

"What about you?" said Leslie, "If you don't mind me asking."

"Like I said, suburban ennui. I had a mum, adopted. She was a nice lady, but it was all so clueless, ya know? Just drift along, imagine nothing was happening, like we could ever have something normal?

Then my best friend joined the Navy and never came back. So I left, thought I'd find something real. I've been in and out, some hard times, but you learn to adjust."

"She's being modest," said Sharon. "Katy's a wizard. She can find anything anytime. I would never have survived without her."

"Someone had to step up."

"What life can throw at us," said Leslie. "You know, I woke up yesterday with a job and house and a life, and by midday I was being hunted by the law, naked and bleeding in an alley, ripping chips out of my body with blunt instruments."

"Mood," said Katy.

"This one's a keeper," agreed Sharon.

"But what about the cops?" said Leslie. "They were after me. I dunno if they're still looking. But we're on the street, and people who look like us ..."

"Yeah, well, most of the cops are men," said Katy. "So you know."

"What do you mean?" asked Leslie, suspiciously.

"I mean, bat your eyes, show some skin, whatever it takes," said Katy. "It's the dickless tracys you have to watch out for."

"Yeah, they always want to 'save' you or something," confirmed Sharon. "Like anyone can be saved. Nah, mate, save yourself, I'm right where I'm meant to be."

They kept sitting there as the morning gave way to the ferocity of the midday sun. They were a still point in the busy square.

"How do you do it?" said Leslie. "All this, I mean? Like, how does it actually work?"

"I dunno if I've learned anything much, except the obvious: never trust men," said Sharon. "But Katy's the expert."

"Well, we get what we can here, some money or whatever. Water, we keep an eye out and grab a bottle from the bin; there's no fountains. Washing, in the river, or a couple of places we know an unsecured tap. You have to pay for the public toilets, so that's out. Shopping malls have cameras, they won't let us in. They ID homeless based on gait recognition so we can't get in anywhere respectable. But if you're quick, you can snatch some food from the dumpsters. Lotsa competition, though. There's a shelter down the road, some food and stuff; but the pastor died, so that's pretty much over. And voting out back of the Hall here."

"Voting?"

"Yeah," said Katy, as Sharon smirked. "'Cos they really care about our opinions."

"And what about a place to stay? Is there anywhere safe?"

"Safe? Good luck with that. It's not easy finding empty space."

Leslie thought for a moment. "There might be somewhere closer than you think." She pointed out her SmarticAIte office. "I used to work there, ages ago. Well, yesterday to be precise. It's always been 90% vacant, but it must be 100% now, the company's broke. They locked me out of my house," she continued, "and convicted me of B&E when I tried to get in. So I went on the run. If that weren't enough, they charged me for the legal fees. I couldn't pay—because the company was bust—so they repossessed the house. It's just zombie algorithms now, churning mindlessly away until the servers die. So technically, SmarticAIte owns my house, but they don't exist. So who's going to sort out the legalities? Everyone uses SmarticAIte lawyers. The same thing must be happening all over. My guess, the properties will just stay empty."

"Can you get us in?" Katy's curiosity was piqued.

"I can try."

"What happened to the guys running the thing, did they 'ascend'?" Katy said with air-quotes.

"Nah, I bet they wanted to though," replied Leslie. "They would have loved that, to be among the 'Chosen'."

"Christ what assholes," said Katy. "They could have done something. But they just left."

"Yeah, I really don't get it," said Leslie. "Like, how? How do you do something like that for so long, and just keep it a secret?"

No-one had an answer to that. When the Chosen lifted off for Earth-2, it became impossible to keep it all a secret any longer. The news, the social, was full of speculation. But Leslie knew most of that was rubbish. Mainly because SmarticAIte produced a lot of it. They were contracted to flood the infosphere with every possible take, every scenario, no matter how bizarre. There's no better way to keep people ignorant than to give them all the information they want and leave it to them to sort it out.

On the one hand, no-one missed a few rich folk all that much. Practically speaking, they were entirely dispensable. But at the same time, it did give rather a sense of finality to the whole apocalypse thing. No-one was really trying any more. And it turns out, they never were. The ones who could have done something gave up long ago.

After a long pause, Sharon said, "Look. We're all screwed. The whole frickin' planet is screwed. The rich have gone, they sucked us dry, the dickhead vampires, and got out, the environment's collapsing, and all this"—she gestured vaguely around—"is falling apart. Zombies, the lot of them, just look, shuffling on as if somehow something will change. You know the difference between them and us?"

"Umm, ooh, let me guess—a life?" joked Katy. "Food?"

"A roof?" offered Leslie.

"Nope," said Sharon. "They've got something to lose. And that means, they're holding on to it, grabbing whatever relic of the past can make them think they have hope. Well, we've got no hope. We've got nothing, we got nothin' to lose. Which means ..."

"We're invisible?" said Leslie.

"Oh no, I know this one—we're gonna get raped and die horrible lonely deaths in a stinking alley?" said Katy over Leslie's giggles.

"It means we're the predators. We're the alpha bitches. We're the shape of things to come." She leaped up and yelled out at the discomfited passers-by: "You think you're alive? You think you're alive? You're dead, you're gone, the lot of ya! You're just too dumb to notice. We're the only ones who get it! We're the survivors! We're the end of the line! *We are the motherfucking harbingers of the motherfucking apocalypse!*"

And something shifted inside them. As they looked over the square, they didn't see the haves and the have-nots. They didn't see the cappuccinos in brand-name cups, or the haircuts or the friendships or the flirting. They didn't see anything that they wanted. They saw only the line. The bright shining line between what is and what is to come. And they stood sharp and clear on the far side of that line while everyone else was fading out, becoming ghosts.

Sharon took the other girls by the hands and said to them, "I already lost one sister to this apocalypse. I'm not going to lose another. It's the end of the world. Are we going to let it beat us? Or are we going to look it in the face and say, 'Yeah nah, piss off'? Are you with me?"

"Kenoath mate, I'm with ya," said Katy.

"What the hell, who even are you people?" said Leslie. "Whatever, I'm in."

"Whatever happens," said Sharon, "we stick together. No 'final girl' crap. The three of us, giving the finger to the apocalypse. It won't know what's hit it!"

"Let's own this shit!" said Katy.

"Woo-hoo!" enthused Leslie.

They sat there for a while feeling powerful. Until Katy said, "So ... now what?"

"Well ..." said Sharon. "Maybe we should start a band?"

———————————————

It was a terrible idea. Which meant it went off like a bucket of prawns in the hot sun. Katy found a busted up old guitar somewhere and she taught Leslie some beats on a wheelie bin. Sharon fronted them with a sneer. They'd head down to the town square, or some mall, anywhere they could make some noise before getting kicked out. What!? Girls gotta get their fun on somehow. Admittedly, the fine art of trash rap was perhaps not the escapist balm needed to soothe those troubled times. One passerby described them as sounding like "three chooks yabbering in the yard". But they were not ones to be stopped by indifference, scorn, or the occasional egg in the face.

Despite their reputation or lack thereof, their songs were really quite educational. Here's their signature tune; it's all about science.

She got them *killing curves*
Never seen such *killing curves*
You want them *killing curves*
You can't stop them *killing curves*

She so hot *whadup with that*
Yeah she fire *whadup with that*
She burn all night *oh yeah all right*
Oh yeah all right *oh yeah all right*

She got them *killing curves*
Never seen such *killing curves*
You die for them *killing curves*
You can't stop them *killing curves*

Heyo folks, listen up, we're the Harbingers. And we're here to rock your apocalypse. It's here and it's coming for you. Have a nice day!

Atmospheric calculations at the Mauna Loa station
Gotcha hyperventilating at the deadly implications.
The math's not hard, it's CO_2 plus two,
Solve for the equation X scares you.
Does danger turn you on? Cos ya bout to go to horny jail.
I know why you sweat, why you quiver and quail.
Creeping down your back, crawling in your dreams,
What if things are really what they seem?

Add one column, take it from the other,
I'm what's left, the unreconciled remainder.
An externality, not quite real—
I am the art of the green new deal.
I'm Shroedinger's rat, biologically squeaking,
You're naturally selected for existential freaking.

Wriggle, giggle, squiggle, twitch.
Patch it up, with Blu Tack and a stitch.
Rub it in, tell me why I'm in the ditch.
Add it up, agree it's nothin' but a glitch.
In the end there's no denying: science really is that
bitch.

She got them *killing curves*
Never seen such *killing curves*
We die for them *killing curves*
We can't stop them *killing curves*

killing curves
killing curves
killing curves
kee – ling – cuuurves!

Having brought it to a banging end, they stood as the passers-by continued on their way, steadfastly ignoring them. Sharon turned to her friends smiling, and nodded in quiet satisfaction. "Appropriate," she said.

after the dissolution

to cast a light in hidden places

Leslie clicked and clicked, but it just wouldn't light. "Got a lighter?" she asked.

"Ahh, no, none I can see," said Katy. Sharon shook her head.

"So ... where can we get one?" asked Leslie. They'd been raiding the shops around Parramatta. Most of the obvious targets had been looted, but there was still stuff around if you knew where to look. They had some regular shops, some warehouses or stores that they knew of. There was no shortage of stuff, not yet at any rate.

———————————————

As the apocalypse started to bite, people seemed to disappear. It wasn't what you'd think, warring gangs or piles of bodies on the streets. There just wasn't anyone around.

Anyone with a car had gotten out, heading for some rumored Shangri-La or safe haven. There were stories of oceans blooming in the desert and cities springing up beside sparkling rivers. The siren song of the interior, long shunned by civilized folk, proved hard to resist. It couldn't be worse than here.

So they packed up their loved ones and their things and they set out for a new home. "No, Johnny, your goldfish wants to stay here, he'll be fine. Come on, we've gotta get going. It'll be fun!" Johnny may have been only five, but he was no fool.

They emerged from the muggy hills of the coast into clear air and flat terrain. Across empty vastnesses they drove. The sun burned harder and the horizon shrank farther. The sky was harsh as neon on steel.

Funny how it got to you, always thinking there'd be something past the next turn or over the next rise. But in the unfurling of the days there was no turn, no rise, just endless straight flat dead miles. Then an abandoned village or a deserted home, burned down or half-swallowed by drifting sand. The sun fried off the face of the land and melted the colors. And still the horizon called, insatiable.

Did you glimpse a figure off the roadside—a tall woman shrouded all in white? She was draped in a long gown, with white gloves and a scarf over her head. Only her face was visible, and it too was white as a mask. She felt familiar somehow, like she had stepped out of a childhood dream; but you couldn't quite put your finger on it. You turned to look, but she was gone. You were about to ask whether anyone else had seen her, but you caught yourself in the nick of time. Soon you told yourself that you had seen nothing, for there was nothing to see. There was no sign of her passing, unless it was the beating in your chest.

There was something numbing in the onward rush. Rationally, you knew you couldn't go on forever. But there was nowhere to stop, no landmark or distinguishing feature. There was no point at which you might say, "Hang on, this was a bad idea, let's go back." So you kept going. There must be something there. There *must* be.

Little Johnny grew restless, and it was only a matter of time until the dreaded words were spoken: "Are we there yet?" What do you say to that? How do you tell a five year old that there is no "there"? That there is only here, and "there" is just a here that we're chasing?

You began to forget where you came from and where you were going. Your mind drifted, lacking definition. You had to make an effort to tell apart the days, to distinguish past from future. Too much effort, it hardly seemed worth it. Someone said something, and you turned, for a moment forgetting who these people were. You said nothing in reply, and just sat beside each other awkward as strangers.

Inevitability settled in your heart. The land had been there all along. You thought it had been conquered, but it was just biding its time. It had thousands of miles and millions of years, more than enough to swallow a few city fools and their dreams and their shame.

The car was a miracle of engineering, fuelled by the sun, and in theory it could go on forever. But you were not driving in theory, you were driving in torrid heat and wild dust on roads of molten tar or loose gravel.

Eventually, the batteries die and you roll to a stop. As the aircon gives out the car becomes unbearable. You get out with your loved ones and stumble around in a daze. Little Johnny, crazed, runs off into the desert. You feel as if you should follow him or at least call him back. But you just stare blankly. You sit beside the car and wait and pick at a loose thread in your shirt. You have nothing to say.

Reality dissolves in the heat and the thirst. The haze peels off the ground and seeps into your brain. You feel the icy claw of death on your shoulder.

Do you see the woman in white? Does she smile as she offers you her hand? You look into her eyes, mutely seeking forgiveness. But you find no mercy there.

Her hands are cold; colder still is her voice as she whispers, "Would you like to see what is underneath my face?" She takes you by your trembling hands and lifts them to her skin. You feel the clammy shape of her face, and, clasping it in your fingers, you pry it off. Underneath is a second face. It is exactly the same as the first.

And so our harbingers were alone. The only ones left in the city were the losers and the outcastes. The ones no-one cared about.

"I guess we'll have to scout a bit for a light," said Leslie. "Ooh, maybe we can pick up some Clinique!" A stroke of luck: nearby a Myers warehouse had survived, so the harbingers were in the habit of protecting themselves from the vicious winds and scouring dust with fine product. They could get all the stuff from the shops that no-one used to let them into.

Fancy duds, too. No-one thought the apocalypse would be dressed in couture, but here they were. Obviously they had to keep it practical, but since when did practical mean dowdy? It was fun to go through all the old stuff and figure out how to greet the end of days in style. Katy was all black and neon, she was going for a Mad Max meets Blondie vibe. Leslie was very precise, very civilized, everything had to be well-fitted, white—which she somehow kept clean—on a navy or dark grey base, with delicate floral prints. Sharon, on the other hand, had this annoying way of just throwing on a plain top or whatever, but it always looked elegant.

"Sure, we can look," said Sharon. "But they'll run out eventually. We'll have to figure out how to light a fire ourselves."

"Okay, well, why not now?" said Leslie. "Katy, you're the clever one, show us how it's done."

"Now I'm the clever one? I thought I was the lazy one," said Katy. "Anyhoo, can't be that hard."

They had a stack of fire-stuff: branches and leaves, or useless furniture or whatever from ruined buildings.

"Too easy," she said. She arranged grass and leaves, with some sticks nested above, and started rubbing two sticks together. The others looked on curiously. Katy rubbed hard and fast but the sticks didn't seem to do anything. "So?" she glared. "You try!"

Sharon and Leslie laughed and hopped to it, each trying their own method. Leslie got some dry grass and a couple of stones, and tried to chip a spark alight; but the few sparks just sputtered ineffectually. Sharon took a log and a hard stick; and in a hollow in the log, began twirling the upper stick. Spinning hard for a few minutes, she was gratified by smoke emerging from the hollow; but it proved hard to translate that into actual flame.

By now they were all sweaty and grumpy. It was near the end of the day. They hadn't yet transitioned to a fully nocturnal existence. But the sun was raging, even low in the sky; and the irony of being unable to make fire in such heat, when fire was consuming the whole world, was not lost on them.

"Stuff it, who cares?" said Katy. "It's too bloody hot anyway."

"But we need fire," protested Leslie. "It's like the foundation of civilization."

"And so, how's civilization working out for you?" jibed Katy. "Fun while it lasted."

"Yeah, well, okay, maybe we took it a little far," admitted Leslie.

"Little piggies in their houses of straw, playing with kerosene."

"Well to be fair," said Leslie, "straw bale homes are pretty fire resistant!"

"We had some in my town. No, super-helpful they were, really," cut in Sharon. "Ashes like everything else. Which, to get back to the subject at hand, is something we'll have to watch out for. We don't want to burn our own house down."

Their shelter was semi-exposed, a couple of floors up, under fifty floors of concrete, in what used to be Parramatta town square. Leslie used to work there, in a swanky office upstairs. Now it was stripped bare, scoured of walls, windows, coverings or furniture, mostly just concrete floors and pillars. But the structure was sound; there was enough shelter from the worst of the winds, while the many concrete slabs above them kept them a little cool.

They waited for a while, letting the problem percolate between them. Eventually Sharon had an idea. "Oh, okay, didn't they used to have a hearth? Like a fixed shelter for the fire, and a bed of coals they kept glowing? I think you cover it over with ash or something."

"Right, yeah. A hearth," said Katy. "So you don't have to light it every time. Nice one, Shaz."

"Hey sweetie?" said Sharon.

"Hmm?" said Katy innocently.

"If you call me Shaz again, I'll feed *you* to the fire."

Anyway, with Leslie's assent, a decision was reached. They got together some concrete blocks, enough for a meter square. Inside they laid wood, stacking it somewhat high, with plenty of kindling.

"Still nothing to light it with," said Leslie.

"This thing's useless," said Katy, as she struck the lighter one more time just to show it didn't work. But as if to spite her, it lit. "Yikes! Okay, let's do it ..." Quickly she laid the flame at the kindling, and it leaped alight.

99

It was hot work, but they kept gathering hardwoods and laying them down, building a solid bed of coals. And when there was enough ash, they laid it on the fire, keeping its glow hidden within.

"I think it was Hesta, Hestia," said Katy, "the goddess of the hearth."

"May she always protect us," said Leslie. "The last light of the old and the first of the new."

"To cook our food and boil our water," added Sharon.

"To keep us safe in the dark and cast a light in hidden places," said Katy.

They paused, suddenly awkward. Katy burst out laughing. "Did we just say a prayer?"

"Maybe, yeah," smiled Leslie. "It was sweet!"

"Well, that's enough religion for me," said Katy.

"Isn't fire one of the oldest of the gods?" said Sharon. "Maybe we should never have stopped praying. We thought we'd tamed the gods. Turns out they were just nursing old grudges."

"Isn't that what we're doing now, though?" said Leslie. "Taming fire?"

"I guess so," said Sharon. "Like our ancestors."

"Except they didn't know where it would end up," said Leslie.

"Neither did the gods," added Katy. "They must have been royally pissed."

"Yeah, we really let them down," said Sharon. "Some children we were."

"Speak for yourselves," objected Leslie. "I was alright!"

"If you say so, little Miss Donut," laughed Katy.

"That's so mean!" said Leslie, throwing a stick Katy's way.

Dodging it, Katy ruminated, "Prometheus stole fire from the gods, right? Zeus punished him by binding him to a rock and feasting on his liver in the form of an eagle."

"Harsh," said Leslie.

"I dunno," said Sharon. "Seems lame compared to ... well this. Maybe Zeus had a point."

The night had fallen around them and the firelight shone on the faces of the three girls, women now, sitting in a circle around their fire. It danced in their eyes and on their skin. Without meaning to, they had slowly assumed the mien of wild goddesses themselves: fierce and dauntless, wiry, with spiky, rough-cut hair.

They had gotten used to the rhythm of taking on the impossible, one miracle at a time. But there was fear there, too. They were so very alone. Horror and despair were never more than a skin's thickness away. They survived together, always together. Never expecting anything, never attaching to anything, always adapting, always changing. One by one, they unlearned the lessons of civilization and learned anew the lessons treasured by their ancestors. It was all so fragile. One mistake and they were done for.

They had to stay alert, to come alive to the sounds and the smells, to seek out meaning in the wind and sense danger in the water. They'd become hyper-vigilant, their senses sharp, able to get by on scraps.

But as they sat together, Sharon realized that none of that was what really mattered.

"No," she said, interrupting their reverie. The others looked expectantly. "No!"

"No ...?" wondered Leslie.

"No, Zeus didn't have a point!"

"Ahh, okay. Well, glad you've solved this pressing issue of Hellenic theology!"

"You'll never survive by punishment, by blame," explained Sharon. "It's love. Love! I love you, you weirdos! You absolute bloody beauties! You goofy dorks! That's how we made it so far, and that's what'll keep us going. Love is what makes it all work, when nothing at all works. It's love."

They didn't know what to say. They sat there awkwardly until Katy said, "Well duh," and jumped right over the fire, to tackle them both in a huge ginormous hug.

the other chris

He couldn't take another step. Then he did. The next step was just too impossible, the deadly weariness in every pore, the overwhelming longing to just sink down and rest. But he did it anyway. And step after step, each one an Everest or a prize-fight, he inched forward through the dust.

The heat was just incredible. And the dust-storm raged like a hurricane from hell. The heat and the abrasion and the gusting, he felt like his skin was being blasted off him.

He could see only a few meters ahead. It was all a swirling mass of greyish-orange. From the heat and from the dim light, he knew it was daytime. And he knew he had to find new shelter after his old was flooded. And soon. Like, real soon. He wouldn't last the hour.

The heat and thirst, the hunger and exhaustion had stripped away his humanity. He couldn't think, couldn't remember, couldn't connect with any spark of his former self.

He used to be a doctor, not long out of med school, just a couple of years in practice. For someone like him, it was a huge deal. He'd always been a smart kid, but he was a loner, and never seemed to make strong connections. But he loved healing, loved being able to serve others, to be part of the process of putting things back together.

He liked his patients and they liked him. They came to his clinic, a simple place which might politely be described as "homely", from all kinds of backgrounds, with all kinds of stories. He listened well, learned the difference between physical and emotional distress, and by and large he did his best. He often said that his job was not to heal, but to witness the process of healing. He just helped his patients stay out of the way.

Then the world ended.

He thought he could be of some use, he thought he could save some people. But they just kept dying. Of hunger, of thirst, of fire, of flood, disease, violence. Over the years he thought less of being a doctor, and more of just getting by for one more day. He had been with people, with communities and groups, but one way or another they had all fallen apart. For the last couple of years he'd been alone. And lonely. What use is a doctor when everyone's dead?

To be honest, he didn't really know how he survived. Got lucky, maybe. Somehow he stumbled from calamity to disaster and came out the other side. Until the storm came, fiercer than ever, waves crashing over his little home right out of the blue. Or out of the greyish-yellow. Metaphors didn't really work anymore. Whatever. More to the point, he'd almost drowned.

Now he was barely walking. Stumbling to make one more step.

But then ... what was it? A shape, looming, like a man. A few metres away, no more. Then it vanished. He—he vanished. Looking, he forgot to stand; he didn't have the energy for both. So he fell. But a strong pair of hands caught him and held him fast.

———————————————

He woke, and the wind had gone and the heat had abated.

"Water," he croaked, and the man brought him water. He lifted him up a little and held the cup gently to his lips.

"Here, lie down," he said, "don't take too much at once." And he laid the helpless doctor down. As he drifted off to sleep, the other man tenderly cleaned his wounds with water and cloth and anointed his raw skin with soft oil.

Again he woke, this time with a measure of energy. The air was clear and he could see the other man huddled over a fire, cooking something. The man got him up and said, "Here, you need to eat." He chewed, each bite painful. But the food wasn't bad; somehow the other man had found some baked beans.

They sat and ate and looked at the fire.

"I'm Chris," said the former doctor.

"Shit," said the other. "Me too. The last two men, and we've got the same bloody name. And some people say God has no sense of humor. Said."

"My place was flooded. A tsunami, I guess."

"Yeah, that was a mother of a storm. I was caught out in the wind, just getting back to my cave when I ran into you."

Dr. Chris looked around for the first time. It was a spacious cave, receding into the sandstone. The floor was soft, white-gold sand. The opening, unusual for this area, was narrow, so you could get good shelter. All around was the furniture of survival: tarps, tins, some rough shelves. Packages on them, maybe seeds? The more he looked, the more impressed he was. There were tools, some wood, pots and pans. It looked like this guy had managed to keep it together pretty well.

Other Chris put out his hand, took the now empty dish. They were full, at least as full as you could be these days. He took them over to one side, and Dr. Chris noticed, for the first time, that there was a live spring of water here. Still dripping! Other Chris washed the dishes with a little water and stacked them neatly.

"You can stay here," he said. "I've been alone a while now and it's not getting any easier. Can you work?"

"Yeah I can work."

"Good."

There wasn't much that needed saying. Dr. Chris allowed himself to imagine that this might work out. Maybe together they could get by for a while.

Other Chris looked outside. It was a new day, looked like, the dawn just fresh. "I'll need to get out and look for some tucker, see if any veggies made it through the storm. You stay and rest up some more, there's no hurry. Who knows what today will bring, huh? Could be a beauty, could be we turn the corner. Gotta have hope, it can't stay bad forever. I mean, we all know, the climate's always been changing, right?"

He looked back at Dr. Chris, pretend casual, but he couldn't hide the sudden scrutiny in his eyes. It took a moment to register; but when it did, Dr. Chris felt his veins turn to ice. Here he was: weak, helpless, trapped in a cave at the end of the world with a fucking denialist.

the possession of a uterus

"Come, my sweet," said Sharon by the fire. "Enough, come and sit with us already. Get out of the wind."

"Mmm, ta," said Leslie, snuggling close. The fire was warm and crackling, clean of fuel and flame. It was the coolest part of the day, just before dawn, when they had their meal. Work was done, foraging and repairs, and they looked forward to a nightly ritual of food and friendship. Tonight was a good night; they had yams and beans.

"Remember that time by the beach, was it last year?"

"What time?"

"The tide had gone out such a long way, and the seaweed was piled up in clumps."

"Oh yes," Leslie said, laughing as she shifted position. "That was fun. How much did we get?"

"Enough that Katy dropped half of it on the way home."

"Yeah, that was ... a moment."

"And a half. My god, she's always so cool and collected, that one."

"You know I'm right here," mumbled Katy, half-asleep. "Like literally a meter away."

"A metre away yet worlds apart," laughed Sharon.

"Bish," came the half-hearted riposte. "Anyway, how can youse stay awake after a night like today?"

"I'm okay, a bit tired but not too bad," said Leslie.

"Yes, I suppose it was only the end part that was really exhausting. The middle was merely enervating."

"It's all relative, my dear," said Sharon. "Some of us are used to hard work."

"Right. 'Cos standing around giving orders is hard work?" said Katy. That was it: Sharon pulled the covers off Katy and turned her out giggling on the floor.

The three of them had been together a long time now. The give and take was how they did things. They had figured out strategies for coping, even thriving in impossible situations. Now they faced a new choice, one that had the potential to change everything. One thing they never questioned, though: whatever they did, they'd do it together.

"Okay so seriously," said Sharon as they settled down again, "what about tomorrow? What exactly are we going to do?"

"Ohh, please," groaned the chorus, "no way, not gonna happen."

"We've got to talk about it some time. The roosters are back in the henhouse."

"I for one say bugger it," said Katy. "We're doing fine without 'em."

"But don't you sometimes, you know, miss it?" said Leslie.

"Only in my dreams. Then I wake up screaming and give thanks to whatever gods have survived this crapshoot."

"So this is assuming we have a choice," pointed out Sharon. "Which may turn out to be wishful thinking. I mean, it's not like we're in our twenties, amirite ladies?"

"Since when did negative thinking get anyone anywhere?" said Leslie. "I mean, if the worst happens, that's that. But what other hope do we have? I mean, otherwise what's it all for?"

"For this," said Sharon. "For us. If we live for each other, getting by the best we can, taking each day at a time, isn't that a lot already? Is it not enough? Do we have some kind of cosmic responsibility to make up for their mistakes, too?"

"Well," said Leslie, "we can't say it was *their* mistake, can we? We were all there."

"Phhgg," snorted Katy. "Of course it's bloody their mistake. Men were in control, men made the decisions. And here we are, living in their world."

"But not these actual guys," said Leslie, "is it?"

"Umm, yeah it is, who else? The tooth fairy?"

They fell silent. Their usual easy familiarity had edged into something a little more caustic, and they knew from long experience when to cool it. The men could wait until tomorrow. Then they could decide whether to couple up and continue the human race, or just let it slide. After all, it was true that they hadn't seen any other people for years, but who was to say what was happening in the rest of the world? Maybe there was an actual civilization still existing somewhere. So far they had survived okay, maybe others had too.

They were still in Leslie's old office building. On the hottest days, there was a bit of a breeze; and during the biggest storms, the sea never rose this far. At least not yet. Each year it was still getting hotter and the water was still rising.

But they worked hard, looked out for each other, and taught themselves whatever new skills they needed. The brackish water yielded few fish, but there was seaweed and algae, sometimes some yams, and roaches for protein. You got used to it.

It had been a long time since they had envisaged anything other than just this, and they had come to a place of acceptance. It wasn't much of a life, but it was theirs. There was no urgency about it, no real need to look for change. So far, any change they'd known had been for the worse.

Anyway, it's not like the possession of a uterus makes you personally responsible for someone else's armageddon.

in the presence of ghosts

"Welcome," Sharon smiled for the men. "All we have is yours."

It was not meant ironically. "All we have" amounted to a cleared space in a ruined building, with a few scavenged blankets and an occasional drip of water from the ceiling. There was barely shelter enough to shield them from the screeching winds. Yet she meant it, and the guests accepted her offer graciously, in silence.

They took their places around the smothered coals of the fireplace. Though it was early morning they were already sweating. They used to have a thermometer, but it broke. Too hot.

Despite the kindness shown by the hosts, the guests were a little uncomfortable. The hosts did not try to dispel the awkwardness. It was a critical moment, and for now, they were happy to keep the upper hand.

"Tea?" Sharon joked. They smiled and nodded, and she offered them an old mug with warm, brackish water. "If we had sandwiches, I'd offer them, too."

The humor was a power move. She was relaxed, enjoying herself, and the men still had no idea if they would get what they want.

One of the guests cleared his throat and started. "I'm Chris," he said. "And this, unfortunately, is also Chris."

The hosts looked at each other. "No. Seriously?"

"'Fraid so."

"M'dudes."

"Yeah well, we all make sacrifices."

The hosts smiled politely. Such humor was a worn currency in the apocalypse. The sayings of the good old days rang like echoes that had lingered too long. "Good things come to those who wait." "Cheats never prosper!" "A bird in the hand is worth two in the bush." She couldn't remember the last time she'd seen a bird. Language was haunted by a past whose memory was equal parts pain and wonder.

"In any case, we have a ..."

"We know what you are proposing."

"Well," he said, making another stab at humor, "we would have brought flowers."

"And we would have brought tasers."

"Uhh ... look," said one of the Chrises, "It's not like that. We're just here to talk and to hear what you want."

"So you're the good guys, then?"

"I like to think so."

"We've all been raped by good guys," she stated matter-of-factly.

He hesitated, then said, "I used to be a doctor."

"Okay, well, useful skill set, in the circumstances."

"And I," said the other Chris, "was a landscape gardener. Also useful!"

"For your sake, I hope so. But hope has never really done much for us, so we're gonna need something more."

The men had come on a long journey. They looked sapped, beaten. Their home in a cave had not worked out. Things changed so fast; what was today a drip of water, tomorrow was a dry rock. They'd been forced to the coast, despite the ever-present threat of the toxic waters. Entering back into what used to be known as Sydney, they spotted the smoke from the cooking fire and make an approach to the three women who lived there.

112

The host took the next step. "I'm Sharon." Pointing, she said, "Katy, Leslie."

No-one knew what to do next. The women looked the men over. One of the Chrises was done up a bit commando style, army belt and vest jacket over, what was that, an old Pink Floyd t-shirt? The other Chris was kind of nondescript, in nebbish beige and checks. Both of them had brought heavyish canvas tote bags. They felt absurd, like teenagers checking each other out. But there was none of the consequence-free lightness of the young. The past hung thick between them.

"Ladies," said Other Chris. "It is truly an honor to be here. We will try to live up to your trust."

"Well for a start," said Katy, "what's in the bags?" Other Chris smiled, and they opened them up. Inside there were dozens of small packages. Chris pulled one out and carefully unfolded it; it was full of large pale seeds.

"Pumpkin," he said. And gesturing to the packages, "Kale, potato, tomato, oranges, grapes, zucchini, chick peas, alfalfa ..."

"Okay wow," said Katy. "I'm hungry already. Beats roaches."

"Yeah well, there's the small business of actually growing the things," cautioned Chris. "But that's where I come in. It was hard in the mountains, the soil was not great. Here though, maybe we'll have a chance. It's a valley, so maybe some of the river silt will still be around."

As he talked, the hosts shared a glance of understanding and a sigh of relief. A decision had been made.

"You'll stay over there," said Leslie. "We'll get you set up. So far this place has served us well enough."

"Ahh, gotta vote," muttered Katy, getting up and heading outside. The Chrises looked confused, but their hosts offered no explanation.

The guests settled in for the day's scorching, lying down on scraps of cloth and getting what rest they could. Their hosts also withdrew to rest. No-one could last long moving in the heat.

It grew quiet. The only sounds were the distant groans of a dying planet: concrete creaking, waves lurching, ashes sifting, beetles murmuring. And the wind whistling over steel and stone.

The apocalypse wasn't done yet, it was just getting fat. Sometimes it seemed as if it was the only living thing left. As if everything else was dead already, it just didn't realize it.

In truth, the living were fading out. They lived, but could not quite remember why. Their thoughts strayed to things gone: to clear water, to plenty, to the ones they had loved and lost. Their minds were full of words and concepts that had lived too long. And in this new existence, there was not much that needed words.

Over the years, the voices in their heads had become ever more dislocated. They had lost any connection with the present, like an unseen choir providing meaningless background noise, telling stories of a past that might as well have been fiction.

As hosts and guests drifted into a half-sleep, the line between this world and the other faded away. It became impossible to distinguish between the whispers in the head and those caught up on the wind. The voices took on a life of their own, as if an unseen mass of the dead were murmuring, obsessed with the few who survived, envious of life even in such a reduced state.

With the envy came a slow hate, a resentment built on the sure foundations of guilt. The guilty dead, watching over host and guest

114

alike. They had imagined that they would be released from all this. That their deeds would somehow be wiped clean. That they would be caught up in a rapture where all things were forgiven and darkness was erased by light. Or better yet, that they would be blessed with the sweet kiss of oblivion.

Yet here they were, wretched spirits condemned to witness wretched lives. Knowing that all this was their fault, yet still trying to convince themselves otherwise. "We did not know!" they whined. "It's not what it looks like!" "We never meant for this to happen!" "Forgive us, we did no wrong!"

But whether they meant it or not, the fact was, it did happen. And their deeds, unlike everything else, did not fade away and perish. No: their deeds weighed heavy in twisted rebar and rotting concrete, in bright-colored plastic and invisible carcinogens. The wages of greed and denial were laid out beneath the sun, plain to see. It was a small thing in the scheme of things, a passing caress on the skin of existence, a gleam in the eye of fate.

The air grew thick with whispers, as if spirits were pressing close, crowding in to catch a glimpse of this moment. This moment when the men met the women. Here there was, after a long time, a possibility of new life. A promise, perhaps, or a threat.

Neither host nor guest knew them. Yet as they lay there restless in slumber, the voices of the dead crept over them like spiders. And unbeknownest to one another, though the furnace of the day was rising, each of them shivered a little; for the dead moved among them, weeping.

unusually rich soil

"She can never know," said Katy.

"Sure," said Other Chris.

"Nah mate, not 'sure'. I'm serious."

"Alright, Jesus," said Chris. "She'll never know. It doesn't matter, the digging's all shallow anyway. No reason anyone should ever know."

"Never," said Katy.

It all started earlier that morning. It wasn't long after the men arrived, and everyone was still sorting things out. But Katy had one thing on her mind.

"Let's see if we can find a place to do it," she said to Other Chris.

Dr. Chris overheard. "It?" he said.

"There's lots of places," said Other Chris. "We need a *good* place. With a nice bed."

"No you're right," admitted Katy, "'cos I was thinking of a *bad* place."

"Okay you two," chipped in Leslie, "how about just *any* place for starters? Just not, you know, here. It's not like there's a shortage."

"But there is," said Other Chris. "Most places are not suitable at all."

"*Any* place?" said Dr. Chris. "What, right here?"

"Yeah, that's what this country has always needed, more space," helped Katy.

"I just said not here. What about over there?" suggested Leslie.

"Isn't it a bit … weird? And, ahh, public?" said Dr. Chris, looking nervous.

"Hey no way," said Katy. "That's where we lay the kelp."

"What?" said Other Chris.

"Seaweed," said Leslie. "We cook it, when it's around. These days the sea's mostly barren, but you get drifts."

"No I mean, I know you can eat it," said Other Chris. "It's a good source of salt."

"Yeah," agreed Katy. "Soup, stew, whatever, it's all good."

"Yeah, sure, seaweed," said Other Chris, "but we're talking about growing."

"I dunno if you can grow it," mused Leslie. "I mean, how would that even work?"

"Not seaweed," said Other Chris.

"Oh, I thought …" said Dr. Chris, hiding his relief.

"Then why bring it up?" said Katy.

"I didn't?" rebutted Other Chris.

"I think we all heard you," averred Katy.

"Alright, enough guys," interrupted Sharon, shaking her head. "Chris and Katy are talking about growing vegetables. In a bed of earth. Leslie's talking about seaweed. And Dr. Chris is talking about sex." Everyone looked at him.

"Oh, well now, that is confusing," said Leslie.

"Not really," said Sharon. "Anyhow, look, Katy, why don't you take Other Chris and see if you can find somewhere?" Looking pointedly at Dr. Chris, she added, "To grow vegetables."

Other Chris put together a little pack with a knife, some digging tools, a water bottle, a couple of rags, a compass, and a magnifying

117

glass. Leslie looked on, impressed, but Katy just laughed outright. "Okay boy scout, let's go."

Parramatta was built on an alluvial flood plain. The silt had built up over millions of years. There was a reason why it was first settled for farming. Roundabouts was the first farm in the country. And not far away there was also "Experiment Farm", which was not, as you might think, a place for weird science, but where they first tried the idea that a freed convict might be given some land and make a life for himself.

Most of the soil's goodness had, of course, been ruined. Much of the land was built over. A lot of it was poisoned, or the topsoil had been stripped by floods. For building works they had dumped a lot of sand, which was pretty useless. The harbingers had got by so far mostly on tinned and other stored goods, with a supplement of whatever animals they could catch: cockroaches, rats, birds, fish. But that was hard work, and getting harder. Roaches were the only insect in any abundance, and they weren't exactly an appetizing choice.

Katy knew the area, but Other Chris knew gardening.

"So we want somewhere with good soil," he said. "Sunlight, but not too harsh. Water, there has to be water. And not too far from where we're living. We'll start with a little seed, don't use it all at once. See what grows, what thrives. You don't want to fight nature. Grow things where things grow. You'd be surprised, sometimes things just take off. You know, one place I was at, we were up a hill, and down the slope all the tomatoes just started appearing. A whole hillside of them. Turns out, it was the sewage. We were crapping out tomato seeds and well, nature did the rest. Anyway, still tasted great!"

Katy half-listened as they walked along, scouting for a place that might suit. She remembered a little patch, it always seemed overgrown. It wasn't far back from the old hospital, around what used to be Parramatta Park. Ahh yeah, here it was. An acre or so, with walls on three sides, protected from the extremes of the winds. And some shade; not many plants could stand the direct sun all day. Weeds ran rich and wild.

"Okay," said Chris. "Now we're talking." He walked around, slowly, taking the measure of the place. He looked at the angles of the sun, held his finger up to test the breeze, pulled out his compass and checked the orientation. He took note of the angles of the leaves, the drift patterns in the soil, the fall patterns of the rain. He stood for a while, just vibing. He looked over the plants, carefully cataloguing what was growing, what was not growing; where it was growing, what was facing where. And what was growing together with what, the pairs and clusters. He took out his knife and carefully cut a stem, watched how the sap oozed.

Katy stared around. They just looked like weeds to her.

Noticing his t-shirt, she said, "So *Back in Black*, is that like a Blackpink cover band or ...?"

"What?" he said. "Are you kidding? No! What's Blackpink?"

"Just a bunch of awesome girls who made the world's biggest K-pop band."

"Well, okay" he said, "but *Back in Black* is AC/DC. And no offence, but I really don't see a girl group rocking hard enough to do it justice."

Katy had him just where she wanted him. "Oh really? And why is that?"

119

"Look I'm just saying. They shred is all."

"Y'know, I used to play a little guitar myself, back in the day."

"Really, cool."

"Yeah. I joined my first professional band when I was thirteen."

"Wow, how'd you swing that?"

"I played *Thunderstruck*."

Oh yeah, that's the look she was waiting for. Bursting out in laughter, she said, "Sorry mate, it was just too tempting."

Chris just nodded along. "Alright then. You got me! And may I say, nice."

While they chatted, Chris was feeling the leaves, looking at the gloss, the green. He stayed as still as he could, to see the insects, the way they moved. Finally he knelt down and gently touched the soil.

"It's good," he said. "Rich, even a hint of moisture." He picked up a clump of soil and, no kidding, inspected it with his magnifying glass. "It's all about the soil structure. This is good, complex."

He looked up at Katy, smiled, and said, "This is a good place. Let's do it. Let's grow a garden!"

They hugged, the first moment of pure affection between the men and the women. A bit awkward, but that's to be expected.

"That's all super-impressive," said Katy begrudgingly. "Really. But I wonder, like, why?"

"Well, I've been doing this a long time," said Chris. "I did land-scaping, not veggies, but the idea's the same."

"Not that, I mean, why this place? Why is it so fertile?"

"Hard to say," said Chris. "Could be anything. But an unusually rich soil like this—there must be something in it."

"What, like fertilizer?"

"Not likely. Chemicals would've leached out by now. Something organic."

Katy looked thoughtful. "Organic?"

"Yeah, like decaying leaves."

"Or flesh."

"Ooh dark, I like it! But yes, flesh," grinned Chris.

"Hey, can we, like, dig a little?" asked Katy. For once, she didn't seem to be joking.

"Sure, of course, there'll be a lot of digging."

"No, like now. Dig down."

"Ahh, okay, but why?"

"Just a feeling."

They pulled out a couple of trowels and started digging. Down a meter or so, the trowels hit something solid.

"Ahh, here's the sandstone," assumed Chris. "Or concrete I guess."

"Hope so," said Katy and kept digging. It was too round for sandstone. They tried to pry it up. It was too hard, so they kept loosening the soil. They saw a white color peeking through. Eventually they pulled it up. A skull.

"Shit," said Chris. "Poor bugger."

"I think we've just discovered the secret of the soil," said Katy.

"What? No," said Chris. "a body isn't going to make much difference."

"I don't think it's just a body," said Katy. "What're the odds that we dig at random and turn up the only skull? See that?" She pointed at a large ruined building nearby. "It's the old hospital. Towards the

121

end, it was just a rendering factory for the plagues. Rumor had, they ended up just dumping the bodies in mass graves."

As it sank in, Chris looked around, "All these plants ..."

"All this soil ..."

"If you're right, there must be hundreds of bodies."

"Thousands. I was around at the time. We saw the operations, it was industrial."

They looked at each other. "We're not going to find anywhere better," said Katy. "But this is bad."

"Yeah," said Chris. "Well, that's what turns sand into soil really, just decaying organic matter."

"No, you don't understand," said Katy. "It's Leslie. Or more to the point, her boyfriend."

"Leslie has a boyfriend?"

"No my dude, Leslie doesn't have a boyfriend. No need to look so threatened."

"I wasn't, it's not like that," blushed Chris.

"It's okay, you like her more than me," teased Katy.

"No, that's not ..."

"Ahh so you do like me? Anyway, not the point. Leslie's boyfriend died. Here."

"Oh," said Chris, then as he realized, "Oh!"

"Yeah. It was just when the plague turned really bad."

"You think ... ?"

"I do. But that's not the bad part," said Katy. "Leslie blames herself. She was one of the early spreaders. It wasn't her fault, but she'll think she killed them all. This whole field, her dead."

"That is awkward," said Chris.

"Ya think?"

"What to do?"

Katy thought for a while, and said, "She can never know."

Chris was right: the ground really was fertile. He took his time, carefully clearing, carefully tilling, carefully planting. It wasn't long before the first tomatoes were ripe.

He gently plucked half a dozen fruit and brought them back for the others. They came together and sat in a circle, like a sacrament. Each of them had a single tomato.

"Chris," said Sharon, "thanks. After all this, you still found that the earth is willing to give. There's still life left in her. We are so grateful to you, and to Katy for finding such unusually rich soil."

They bit into the ripe, red tomatoes. Juice spilled as the luscious, vibrant taste filled their mouths. Leslie closed her eyes in appreciation. Katy couldn't help but whimper a little. Years of cockroaches and seaweed and tinned chick peas will do that to you.

They started laughing.

"Oh my God, that is so good!"

"Wow, so sweet!"

"Juicy!"

"It has that richness, the umami."

"Yeah, that'd be the corpses," chuckled Katy.

They stopped and looked at her.

"Oh no," she said.

an efficient solution

Leslie didn't need much sleep, so she always got up before the others. The sun burned low over the ruins and the river, but it had not yet vanished. It was still too hot, really, but Leslie shook it off. She was used to it. She even liked it somehow; at least it was something.

She took her time getting dressed. It was part of her daily ritual, helped her to keep things together.

Then she checked around the camp, tidied what needed tidying, putting things in their place. It wasn't exactly homely, but you had to keep some kind of order.

She checked the basic supplies: wood, grass, cloth. All seemed fine. Only water. Every day, water must be fetched. It was a familiar routine, boring as most things in the apocalypse: a couple of metal pails; a pole to hold them; a pad of cloth for her shoulders. Finally, her secret blade. She didn't need it every day, but it was a comfort to have it by.

She stepped down the stairs and picked her way along the well-worn path. Each step built the pressure in her guts. It was like a living thing, a gnawing necessity, an animal twisting inside her. She never knew which would win: her will or the creature.

By the river she settled and drew her water. It was a simple task; and if the water was full of scraggle and brack, she knew how to purify it. Leslie could always figure out stuff like that. She kept herself busy. That was why she did this little job herself; she was good at it. She enjoyed being of service, always had. It was almost an accident that it gave her a chance to be alone every day. To reclaim her privacy from the ones she loved.

The men had settled in, they were working out okay. It was a different dynamic, to be sure. There was so much that passed them by. She couldn't understand how they could be so oblivious. There was a whole world of hidden communication that passed among the women, and the men didn't even know it existed.

As she squatted down by the shore, she inspected the scratches on her feet and ankles. She always laughed it off in front of the others, "Clumsy feet!" Which was odd, because she was normally so precise. But there were so many thorns, stray bits of wire, jagged edges. With all the chaos, a few cuts were no big deal. Her friends never noticed; they were too close to see.

She touched the scars tenderly, almost lovingly, her fingers sensing the delicate heal of the old cuts and the raw scabs of the new. Runes etching her story in her skin. They were pretty in their own way, but most of all, they were hers.

The pressure snapped and rightaway her will vanished. She double-checked no-one was around, then took out the blade. It was an efficient solution.

On her way back, she ran into Dr. Chris. She smiled brightly, "Hey."

"Here, let me help you with that," he offered uselessly; the pails were well balanced and secure, one at either end of the pole, and her shoulders were strong. But she was happy to walk together a while.

"It's okay," he said.

"Sorry?"

"You're lucky," he said. "You look after each other so well. Even before, how many people found their family like you have?"

"I know!" she said. "God I love them so much. We kept each other alive and sane. Mostly!" she laughed.

"Mostly," echoed Chris, and they walked a little further.

"You know, coming down here is always hard for me."

"Oh?" she said. "I think it's nice."

"Yeah, I used to love the river too. But ... well, something happened."

Leslie paused, then said "Tell me."

"You won't like it. I was not exactly the hero."

"Who needs heroes? We just need survivers. You must have saved a lot of lives."

"Not this one," said Chris. "I was living with a small community up near Gosford, a couple dozen of us. The water still had fish then, and we were doing okay. One of the guys used to climb the cliffs looking for eggs. Well, one day it went wrong. He slipped and fell, and I happened by, I heard him screaming. It was bad. His leg was shattered, bone everywhere, blood pooling. In the old days, yeah maybe we could save him, even reconstruct his leg. But now? All the time and effort, and he'd probably die anyway?

"But I'm a doctor. It's my job to try. I should have tried to set the leg, staunch the bleeding." You could see the pain fresh in his eyes. "I told myself it was a medical decision, that there was no hope. But it wasn't. Not really."

He fell silent. Somehow they had stopped walking. Leslie put down the buckets and pole to listen. "It was like a click in my mind. A moment of envy. I wanted out. I didn't want to heal him, I wanted to *be* him. I wanted to hurt like that, to feel death coming and know what life was worth. So I left him there. To die alone. God I was so close. Not to saving him, that was never an option. No: what I wanted more than anything was to jump and die by his side. It was all I could do to just walk away. Back at camp I pretended I hadn't seen him, and by the time the group found the body it was too late."

He looked at Leslie and bowed his head, "So that's me. The doctor who envies the dying."

Leslie heard him out, recognition in her heart. "I get it. The pain is what keeps it real."

Chris hesitated and said, "You can talk to me, you know. Doctor-patient confidentiality and all that."

A little tightly, Leslie said, "What have we got to hide?"

"What indeed?"

They were about to start walking back when Dr. Chris said gently, "Leslie, give me the blade."

She looked at him in shock, "What?"

"You hid it well, but I'm a doctor. The cuts are too straight. It's not thorns or wire. You have to keep the cuts even, to keep control. Just enough to let it out."

Leslie laughed, "Don't be ..."

"Leslie," he said quietly. "Stop. Just give it to me."

It took a moment, but she got there. She slipped out her blade and gave it to him, trembling. "You don't know what I did," she said. "I killed them all. One person? You killed one person? I killed all my friends, my boyfriend, everyone."

"I know," he said. "I know. But you've suffered enough now." He took her by the hands and held her gaze in his eyes. "We have all suffered enough. It's time to let go. Will you come with me?"

She nodded. As they set to go, Leslie bent to pick up the water, but Chris said, "Hang on a tick." He rearranged the buckets, placing them next to each other, and threading the pole so it came out an equal distance on both sides. "Let's try it this way. Maybe it'll be easier." They lifted the pails together, one shoulder on each end of the pole. Together they brought the water back to their friends.

When they got back, Katy greeted them, "Ahh, so you've found a lackey. I knew they had to be good for something."

Leslie laughed, "Well, to be honest, it was easier by myself. But you gotta make 'em feel important."

Chris pretended to be affronted. "You don't need my manly strength?"

"Maybe. Or maybe you have a different superpower," said Leslie. "We'll discover it one day."

The banter went back and forth as they got going for the night. They laughed together as they did the chores. Soon it was day again and they settled in to sleep.

When Leslie woke it was pitch dark. She looked around confused.

"Hey sleepyboots," said Katy. "Just in time, we've finished chores."

"What!" said Leslie. "How long have I been asleep?"

"Long," said Dr. Chris. "You must've needed it. Don't worry, we got stuff done just fine. And you're with us now."

Leslie got up and joined her friends, rubbing the sleep out of her eyes.

the dry wanted breaking

The dry wanted breaking, but the sun didn't care. You could feel the moisture wicking out your skin. It had been so many years, the thought of rain was fading like a memory of childhood, like splashing in the hose on the front lawn. The sky was cast in steel.

Sharon looked around at her friends, her lovers sleeping, at the wreckage and salvage of their things. There was so much that was not there. Still, it was enough. They had each other.

Eliana was sleeping too, and her mother rocked her gently. There was no real reason it had to be Sharon; it just ended up that way. They had, in the end, agreed. It probably wasn't really a thing, in hindsight. Nature will have her way. But Katy had said, "Nah uh," so it was her and Leslie. And Leslie never got pregnant. So it was her. And the father, who statistically speaking was likely to be Dr. Chris. They were never really sure, but that's what they all accepted. Not that it mattered to Eliana; she just called them all "amma", a baby's habit she never outgrew. Roles didn't seem so important any more.

The pregnancy and birth was no harder than it needed to be. Her extended family took care of her, and they had a bona fide doctor. Not that any of them were actually there when she delivered.

Late one morning she couldn't sleep. She got up and felt an inexplicable need to go for a walk. She wandered off, belly be damned, until by accident or fate she came to a strange hidden place. Between one ruin and another, through a forsaken doorway, down a shrinking corridor, and out into an enclosed—well, once it would have been a garden or a courtyard.

The concrete there was crusted black with dirt and oil, but there was a pale thread across it, a whitening of many feet. She wondered who it was that had trodden so often in this secret place. All around was a circle of mirrors. The glass of the derelict offices had not shattered, and for some reason it stayed shiny. In the middle was a straggling white tree, a ghost gum, miraculously not dead; maybe it was fed from an underground spring. It was the last living tree in Parramatta.

The circle of mirrors reflected and amplified the already outrageous sun, while the black ground absorbed heat and radiated it back, hotter. It was like someone had turned on an oven. The air was on fire and the light was blinding even through closed eyes. She leaned holding the tree, bathing in the sun, gasping in the power and the sublimation. She felt transformed, like a phoenix bursting into flame. Suddenly her waters broke and she knew it was happening. Her daughter was born there, in fire.

That was six months ago. She'd made it, and her little girl had made it. Eliana. Here she was, so softly sleeping, in the cleanest and softest cloths they could find. Sharon held her baby, cooing her gently, and singing sweetly a song that, in a world far away and a time long ago, her big sister had once sung for her.

> Lullaby little one,
> sing me to sleep.
> Tuck down the coverlets,
> snuggle in deep.
>
> Tell me a fairy tale:
> princess so fair,

monsters and magic,
and long golden hair.

Daddy is crying,
mummy's away;
but we'll be together,
I promise I'll stay.

Wind in the treetops—
look, there's the moon!
What a funny old feeling,
here in my room.

Sharon looked down at her beautiful daughter, so precious and amazing; and then out at the wreckage of the city, the tumbling smash of steel and stone. She knew where lay her heart. She would always be there for her daughter, as her sister had been for her.

She missed the comfort of tears. The welling of emotion in the gut and the chest, rising to make the face screw up all ugly and surge into the eyes. The tracks of the tears cooling on her face. The shudder in the shoulders. The letting go into vulnerability. The acceptance of the grief and the peace of its passing. It was nice to think of those things. Now they had too many things to cry about, but the well, it seems, had run dry. But she never forgot that once upon a time, she had had those feelings. Once, she too was human.

gods and monsters

They took turns telling stories to little Eliana as she grew up. They shared their thoughts, their hopes, their fears. Of what happened this morning, or yesterday. Or last week. Stories of what it was like Before. Maybe it was a way of remembering who they were.

As time slipped by, the silly stories, the useless ones, were left by the wayside. Facts dimmed like the evening sun, losing their sharp edges and their details. In the night, facts turned into entities, taking on a life of their own, illuminated in the soft light of the imagination. And the stories that survived were the ones that burned brightest in the mind.

It was as if the stories bent the storytellers to their will. No matter where they started from, the stories somehow all wound back to the same question, worrying it, prodding it, never letting it rest. Who were the gods? And what monsters killed them?

The ruins of a lost civilization evoke a sense of wonder like no other. The Buddha spoke of a forgotten city in the forest; it is the statue of Ozymandias, or the temples of Indiana Jones. For the little group, five adults and a single child, huddled in the wreckage of the City of Parramatta, the lost civilization was not just a few pillars, a broken shrine, or a buried wall. They lived among the million acres of brick and steel and bitumen and concrete that the gods left behind. Bridges, freeways, skyscrapers, and the endless wastelands of the suburbs were their jungle, their desert, and their home. There they hunted and foraged, found water, hid from the sun, and raised their daughter. And survived to do it all again tomorrow.

Towards morning, when the scraps of food had been eaten, they would gather around the hearth to share what solace they might. For a while they felt safe and loved. They'd talk, the usual trivia of the day, chat about this and gossip about that. But in the back of their minds, the question whispered, like a shadow in the corner of the eye. They knew it, they feared it, they could not look at it. So they filled the space with chatter and noise and laughter, holding each other close, keeping the shadow at bay as best they could. But it did not take too long for the quiet to fall. And when all else was silent, the question remained.

There are some questions that cannot be answered because you already know the answer. So you don't answer it: you tell a story. You know the story, but you tell it anyway. It is the story of Icarus, the god who flew too close to the sun. Of Mandhātā, the king who wanted the heavens and fell to earth. The story of the gods who became too greedy. You tell it to the child, because it is all you have.

But if you think that you can satisfy a child with a story, you have not met Eliana.

"Didn't they know?" asked Eliana. "They were gods, they knew everything. You told they could just get any answers whenever they wanted."

"Yes, they knew," said Dr. Chris. "The wise and the true among them spoke of what was to come. Their sages spent long years crafting stories, giving them wondrous names like 'IPCC Special Report'."

"How come they didn't listen?"

"Some listened. Many, in fact," added Leslie. "They knew and they watched with horror. They even did a little bit, here and there, to make a difference. They bought a different brand of chocolate, or they expressed their opinion in no uncertain manner, or they pressed a button on a screen in protest. But it was not enough."

"And there were ... others," said Katy.

At this point a chill would fall. No matter how hot the day, this was a cold that stuck in the marrow. Other Chris reached out to Eli, held her hand. He didn't like that they told her such things, but it was not his place to stop them.

"What others?" she said, pretending not to know.

"Monsters. Not human, but passing as human. Vampires: respected noblemen by day, but by night, they changed into hideous blood-drinking bats. They descended on the poor folk of the villages and devoured their very life."

Shivering, Eli protested, "But you told there were only a few vampires."

"It was not just vampires. There were zombies, mindless hordes of the undead, who prolonged their unnatural state by devouring the brains of the living. And trolls, ugly fiends who lurked under bridges, snatching up any fool brave enough to travel those perilous roads."

"If the gods were so powerful, how could the monsters fight them?"

"It was the night," said Sharon. "In those days, not like today, the night was fearful and the day was blessed and warm. The gods were strong in the day, but the monsters waited in the shadows and struck in the darkness."

"So they killed all the gods?"

"That's what some say. But others say the gods ended up being consumed by their own fury. Infected by the reckless evil of the monsters, the gods came to hate them with a boundless rage. They built their greatest machine, and flying in it, they left this world behind on a pillar of fire. Now they live in the sky, snug inside the sun. In the morning they rise and scorch the whole world. They are still trying to kill the monsters. But they don't know that the monsters are long gone, and it is only us that they burn. So we hide in the day, like the monsters of old, and come out in the night when it is cool and safe."

"But what happened to the monsters? How could they all just disappear?"

"Hush, child, sleep," said Leslie. "The monsters are gone now. This is the world they left behind, and now there's just people like you and me."

But that last part was a lie. They all knew it. The monsters were real. They hide in the coldness of the heart, in the cruelty of the passions. They were right there with them, even in the warm circle of the firelight. They have always been there, and we have always known them.

Is it really a question if we already know the answer? Or do we just pretend it's a question so the truth becomes a little easier to bear?

The adults sitting around the hearth at the end of the world are today's children. They tell their child stories of how things came to be the way they are. For her, we will be the monsters. We will be the thing that stalks her in the dark. We will be the beast that hunts her in her dreams and the nightmare waiting beside her bed when she wakes.

She will never understand, not really, why we lived the way we do, knowing what we know. Her deepest fear will be that she will turn out like us, that the same blank unconcern lurks in the depths of her own heart.

They will tell her stories that turn us into monsters so that she can sleep at night. So that, for all the sufferings and hardship she will endure—the hunger, the heat, the disease, the violence and devastation of a world from which all good things have fled—she may cherish some small comfort: at least she is not a monster like us.

And it will work, for a little while. The little girl will fall asleep, soft and sweet as a pigeon's coo.

Until the sun rises once more, and the vengeance of the gods is laid in fire upon the face of the earth.

the marsh's edge

Eliana crouched at the marsh's edge. Stick in hand, she scratched at the mud. Not random, by any means: she was very serious and intent on her work.

She drew lines, crossed them, joined the corners with circles, and made spirals all around. It made something like a flower or a maze; a lily perhaps. But she was right on the water's edge, and the mud was soft and squishy. So as she drew, the water, tepid and briny, lapped over her pattern, wiping it out. That was the game: how much could she draw before it got washed away?

Sharon was just over there, wading in the shallows, looking for yams. It was always yams or leaves or some such that they foraged; Eliana refused to eat any animal. They'd been out since first light, and by now, a couple of hours later, the sun was starting to burn, and the weird heat of the day was pushing in.

Mother and daughter were both covered up well, no skin exposed, hoods pulled down over the face. The girl's dress, tattered though it was, still kept some faded yellow flowers. The dust was almost settled this morning, and her coughing had only a little blood. It wasn't too bad a day, as days go.

Sharon looked over at Eliana, blankly checking that she was still there, still okay. It was all just so exhausting. She remembered that she should love her daughter; believed that, somewhere inside, there must be some kind of love. But it had been ever so long since she had energy enough to feel it. She had no room left for the sweeter emotions. She wondered, briefly, at this; it didn't feel like a lack, exactly. It was just normal. It was just how it was. Sometimes she thought she should have something more to offer her child, but the fact of it was she was too tired to feel guilty. The sun had burned all her love away, and now the best she could do was this.

Eliana, still scratching, turned up a worm. She stopped and looked at it, wriggling softly, all grey belly and slime. It turned about, looking for a way back into the easy marsh. She leaned forward and, ever so carefully, picked the worm up in a handful of mud. Moving downstream a little, she placed it back where it belonged, in a nice, untouched bed of soil. She watched as it wriggled itself back under the earth.

Noticing her mother watching, Eli looked up and waved shyly. Her mother's eyes filled with tears, deep and silent, at the unaccustomed feeling she felt within. In wonder, she realized: this is joy.

on fire they descended

On fire they descended, a pillar of fire, a sea of fire, a monstrosity of fire.

It was the middle of the day but the roar woke them up. "What the!" said Katy.

Leslie jumped up and picked her way to the building's side, peering out through the dust, now billowing in clouds even thicker than usual. She saw it: from the terrible blaze of the sun, a smaller flame detached itself. As it came closer, she saw it was a little metal pod balanced like a toy on the massive tower of flame, slowly settling to earth.

"Holy shit," she yelled. "They're back!"

"No," said Other Chris. "No frickin way."

"Or it's aliens," said Katy helpfully. "Do you think it's aliens, Chris?"

"Really?" he said. "Now?"

Smirking, Katy was about to get in another dig when Eliana broke in, "What is it?"

The adults looked at each other. Their policy was to never hide anything from the kid. But this—well, it was a lot.

Breaking the stalemate, Sharon took Eli's hands and said, "It's the vampires."

Eliana's eyes went big.

Dr. Chris reassured her, "It's not like the stories, I promise. They won't drink your blood or anything. They're just people. Only, you know, rich assholes who left us for dead."

"But why'd they come?" wondered Eliana. "Isn't everything all fancy and nice where they are?"

No-one had an answer to that. Wrapping themselves up, they made their way outdoors and trekked the short distance to where the pod had settled. Hidden behind some rubble, they watched as the doors opened and people stepped out. They seemed so befuddled, disorientated. Leaning on each other, covered in some kind of shiny suit, with helmets so you couldn't see their faces.

"They don't look like much of a threat," said Other Chris, and for once everyone agreed with him. Breaking cover, they made their way down on to the flat where the pod had perched at an awkward list.

The vampires—people—slowly filed out and gathered by the pod doors, waiting for them. There were a couple dozen. The six survivors approached them until they stood in a group opposite. There was no sign of aggression, no apparent need for fear. Then, as if at a sign, the newcomers started unclipping their helmets. They pulled them off to reveal their faces.

"Oh!" exclaimed Eliana with the gracelessness of a child. "They're so *white!*"

―――――――――――――――

The apocalypse, for all its flaws, at least had a sense of irony. It was white people who had dug the coal and pumped the oil that fuelled the fires that drove the machines that made more machines that dug more coal that ended the world. And it gave them power. And with that power they conquered the world and spread their

140

fire and their lies and their machines everywhere. Until people the world over forgot who they were and burned their own coal to drive their own machines to dig more coal, just like the white people had taught them. And on and on it went, but always the white people were there, skimming the fat.

With the power and the money that the machines gave them, they lived in clean bright cities and sent their rubbish to dirty places full of poor brown people. And when those poor brown people got on boats and tried to find somewhere to live, the white people sent out bigger boats and shot them dead right there in the water.

But they couldn't hide from the sun. Not forever. As fires consumed region after region across the globe, spectacular pyrocumulonimbus cloud systems formed in great towers, driving tens of kilometers up in the sky, carrying aloft billions of tonnes of smoke. The smoke reacted with the ozone, depleting the earth's protection against UV. Holes in the ozone layer, thought to have been a solved problem, reappeared and spread. As the days grew fierce and the sun became the enemy, people plastered themselves with lotion. But the lotion ran out. They tried to wrap themselves up, to hide from the sky, but you could never hide completely. Just a few minutes direct exposure and they started turning pink. Even ambient sunlight was enough, though it took longer. From pink they turned red, then their skin started to blister and peel. Raw scabby blotches all over their faces and arms, infected and malignant.

The darker your skin, the better your odds. Those with yellow skin or red skin were a little better off, but over time they suffered the same fate.

Our survivors had one thing in common. Regardless of whether their heritage was Aboriginal, South Asian, Melanesian, or African, their skin was black. Dark black. Rich in melanin and roasted in the sun, black skin was the number one prerequisite for survival.

———————————

Eliana had never seen a white person. To her, they looked just like the vampires of the stories: bloodless aristocrats of dubious appetites. "Amma," she said, scared, "Don't let them eat my legs!"

"Your legs?" said Katy. "Why would they ... Oh never mind, shoosh sweetie, they won't eat you. Or your legs." Bending over, she whispered conspiratorially, "But now you mention, they do look rather yummy!"

"Eww amma, no!" said Eli.

"Soft and downy. Mmm, delicious."

"Stop it!" said Eli, but she couldn't help laughing.

While Katy distracted Eliana, Sharon stepped up. "Hello, my friends," she said to the strangers. "Welcome."

The strangers were awkward, unused to everything. They squinted and cowered somewhat, as if the world itself was too much for them. But they came forward, and one of them took Sharon's hand. Holding it in their hands, their plump grasp moist and clammy, they said, "My name is Arixys. We come from Earth-2."

"Here," said Sharon. "Let's get you under some shade."

———————————

They took the strangers in, fed them and sheltered them. Eliana was thrilled; someone else was the baby for once. She took great pride in showing everything to the newcomers.

"Here's the water, we strain it with this. Over there we go to collect yams and things. Cooking here, bathing by the shore, voting next door."

"I'm sorry, what?" said Arixys.

"Voting," said Eliana, confused. Sharon laughed.

"Next door is the Town Hall, used to be anyway. That's where we go to register our dissatisfaction with the political process."

"I'm not sure I understand," said Arixys.

"It's the toilet," said Leslie. "We take a dump on the politicians. Better late than never!"

"It's the least we can do," affirmed Sharon. "Makes us feel, I dunno, like we're giving something back."

"Good to know," said Arixys.

It was like looking after a gaggle of huge babies. They couldn't cook, couldn't forage, couldn't, well, do anything much really.

"What's up with that?" said Katy in her usual diplomatic manner. "The whole, get through life lacking basic survival skills thing you've got going there."

Arixys was too exhausted to take offence. The heat was too much. They and the other vampires, as Katy liked to call them, were lying about like seals on a beach. Used to.

"The machines took care of us," they said. "We were fed and clothed, and could focus on higher things. Or so we told ourselves. Actually there was a lot of gossip and, well, self-stimulation."

"You had machines doing everything?"

"Yes, they were like our servants. Except they never got tired or took a day off."

"So," chimed in Leslie, "what happened to them? They must be at a loose end. Are they still up there, cleaning your empty houses?"

"Ahh, yeah," said Arixys, exchanging awkward glances with some of the other arrivals. "There was a bit of a bug there. A design flaw of sorts." They obviously didn't want to go on, but it's not like Katy gave them a whole lot of choice.

"Okay, so no, they don't stop. Ever. They are self-repairing, self-replicating automatons guided by sophisticated AI. Their design imperative was to ensure humanity had all its needs satisfied. When that's done, in their down time they repair themselves and make new machines. They are programmed to hunt for resources and turn them into raw materials for manufacture. Their neural nets keep evolving, learning more efficient ways to achieve their basic imperative.

"But humanity stopped needing so much. It was expected that we would grow, that demand and consumption would always require more robots. The Celestial Amazon—the network for producing and distributing goods—was predicated on infinite growth. So when we started ordering less, the machines had time on their hands. Never ones to waste a thing, they started making more robots and consuming more raw materials. To feed a humanity that no longer exists."

"Umm, human existing right over here," piped up Katy, "just in case they have a little extra!"

"Any humans, *except* those on Earth-1, that was how they were built."

"Seriously?"

"They thought you were a lost cause. Sorry."

144

"Okay, so they are still up there, still churning away?" said Leslie. "It's kind of nice in a way, at least humanity has some place in the stars."

"Except, well, you know how exponential growth works, right?" asked Arixys. "One machine builds two, two build four, four eight, and before you know it, there's millions, then billions, then trillions. They were built to mine the asteroid belt, and we always thought that would be enough. But there are so many now, billions upon billions of self-replicating machines, hungry for materials and energy. They have already used up the asteroid belt. They're starting on Mars. Within a few decades, they'll turn all the raw materials in the solar system into copies of themselves. Then they'll set out for the stars. They can't stop; it's not in their programming. They'll just keep going, unless they come up against some superior force: aliens or gods or better robots I guess. They'll just eat the universe. They promised infinite growth; well they delivered."

They just sat there, trying to take it in.

"You mean," said Sharon, "they just ... Oh God. Oh no."

"Well fuck," said Katy.

"It's like, a metaphor or something,' said Other Chris. "The robots are like we were, before. We thought we could just keep on consuming."

"No really, Chris," said Katy. "Explain it for me a little more, I'm not sure I get it." Leslie sighed, but Chris took the bait.

"Well, it's like the robots are consumers ..."

"Chris. It's called sarcasm," said Leslie. "We get it."

"Ohh. Right."

"Anyway, I thought you didn't believe in climate change," said Sharon. Dr. Chris looked horrified and shook his head. But it was too late.

Arixys was shocked. "What? What do you mean?"

"Well no, hang on," said Other Chris, "the climate's changing, obviously."

"Obviously," nodded Katy, enjoying Leslie's glare.

"But what's the cause?" asked Chris, his skeptical energy sounding weary. "I mean, if you do the research, there's a lot of questions. I guess we had something to do with it ..."

"Something?" said Arixys. "The science has been understood for a century or more. How is this still a question among you?"

"It isn't," said Katy drily. "Chris is special."

Chris, trembling, said, "I know what you think of me. I'm not stupid. But I lost everything." He paused. "My wife—oh God, Cynthia, my love, she was everything. My little girl—she ... I couldn't stand it. They were saying—the videos were saying, it's all lies, it's all a conspiracy. I had to find someone to blame. Otherwise ..." and he finally broke down in tears. "Otherwise it's on me. It's my fault, I killed her."

Wordlessly, Katy took him in her arms. They sat there together in silent acceptance, knowing. Katy held him close, rocking back and forth, the only thing that kept him from collapsing in grief. They knew. They all knew.

While they were speaking, the night had dropped from hot to cool to positively chilly. It was rare but not unprecedented; climate change was a fickle bastard. Like a distant zing of ozone, a smell came in the air. Leslie looked up curiously. She noticed from the dim black sky a white dot drifting down, and others behind it. It was snowing! A thing unheard of in Sydney, even in the old days. As the sparse flakes grew thick, coming down in clouds, they gazed out at the sight in amazement, relishing the feeling of being cold. After a while the snow slowed and came to a stop. And a breeze blew the clouds away, revealing a night sky that was clear and a light that shone full from above.

"Oh!" cried Eliana. "Look, it's the moon! It's the real moon!" She jumped up to see. The moon was bright and plump, beaming down as a silver beacon from a world free of pain. And all around it, the Milky Way soared across the sky like a revelation. Except it wasn't really milky; by some strange quirk of the weather, the sky revealed itself on that night with unparalleled clarity. It was a cathedral of colored lights, a vault of infinite heavens, a cascade of bright gems strewn across midnight velvet.

Smiling, Sharon and Dr. Chris took her by the hands, saying, "Yes, it is. Isn't it beautiful? It's just like the song!"

For a moment it felt like maybe things mightn't be too bad. The moon shed her light over land and sea, over the living and the lifeless, knowing no distinction of race or color or country or creed. Once, men strode upon her as conquering heroes and planted the flags of their proud nations. Now those flags were all that remained, while the nations lay in ruins and the last humans gazed upwards in awe, silent before her grace.

Softly her light fell and softly it sparkled in each crystal of fresh-fallen snow that swathed a thankful land. Pearls veiled the bruises of the city, lovely as a bride before the altar. The ruins of St Johns dusted soft with silver, and it seemed as if it might in truth be a mansion of the gods, or a hallow, perhaps, for the churchyard dead whose snow-laden crosses marked their ancient bones. The fallen snow drifted thickly on the crumbledown walls of the old Town Hall, piled lazy in middens on the banks of the fishless river, and beyond, folded the razed remnants of the once-proud city of Sydney in a doona of pure white light and softest down. The night shone forth as a blessing, as if raised up by safe and loving hands in a gesture of redemption unlooked-for.

norm

She didn't really know why she called him Norm, it just happened. Maybe because he kept them on the straight and narrow? If so, he wasn't doing a particularly good job of it! But anyway, there it was. He was Norm, and he was a good boy.

When she was younger she'd throw a stick for him and he'd scamper after it it, bringing it back all sloppy and chewed. And again, and again, until she lost interest. These days they'd still play, but not so often.

Still, Norm followed her everywhere and today was no exception. She felt good, like a decision had been made, a direction had been chosen. She doused cold the dying flame in the hearth, to never burn again.

Picking up her small bag, and checking she had a water bottle, she set out. No need to call him, he was right there. He really was a good boy.

She picked her way along familiar paths, heading onwards and upwards. She knew that there were hills, and beyond them, mountains. And that was where she was going. She'd never seen them, had never ventured that far, but if not now, when?

Some miles into the journey, she remembered, "Oh, I should have said goodbye!" She hesitated, wondering whether to turn back. But reason got the better of her. Her ammas wouldn't mind. They were as happy as Larry, with their beds of lilies and pillows of rose.

The path grew strange to her. The marshy labyrinth had given way to the dry, all ashy gray dirt and fallen thorns. She walked slowly, there was no rush, nowhere to be. Picking out a safe footfall was second nature. She'd never worn shoes. Each step brought her in contact with the earth, reminded her of where she was. There was so much detail in a step, so much information about texture, temperature, materials. Dangerous ground announced itself clearly if your feet were listening.

Behind her grew a soft glow of rich, grainy crimson. She'd have to find shelter before the sun rose. There were no trees, of course, but plenty of broken buildings. She found a nice little niche, and settled down with Norm. He found a puddle of water for them. Hopefully the next night they'd get something to eat.

So they waited out the day and got going again when the air was bearable, around midnight. A few days of this and the ground was rising. They missed the food you could still get in the lowlands: yams and greens, seaweed, and moss. But a couple of derelict buildings had yielded some canned stuff, and the prickly vines had a tart, sour fruit. Anyway, they were used to it. They didn't need much. Norm survived, chasing down a lizard or, on a good day, a rabbit. She didn't like that he killed things, but she knew that was what he ate. It was only natural.

It was the water that was hardest. There were valleys and gulleys where once had flowed broad rivers, cool and fresh, or bright young streams splashing. But the cleansing waters were long gone, and in the riverbeds was only dust, or a black, congealed slime or bog. There was no dew in the morning or rain to be expected. Deep, hard roots were the only thing left, and they yielded little water with much effort. Her skin was thick with dust and sweat.

The ground rose day by day, yet their vantage grew no broader. The air was so thick with ash and dust, you couldn't see more than a few tens of meters no matter how high you were. She tightened her mask and went on, guided by memories of stories.

Uncle Chris had told her about a cave he'd once stayed in, where he'd met her father. "Your father was a good man," said uncle Chris. "He was nearly lost in a dust storm. I saved him and brought him in. We lived high in the hills where the sea could not reach us, in a cave that stayed cool and sheltered from the wind." But they ran out of water and had to leave.

She didn't know more than that, so she just walked. Chances of finding a cave were slim, but so what? It wasn't like there were a ton of options. Without her father, it had got harder for all of them. They had come to lean on him more than they knew. When the white people came from the sky, it was Dr. Chris who had cared for the sickly guests.

It took a while for the story to come out. The white people were almost comically unable to function. They gasped at the air, fainted at the heat, groaned at the lack of food. Yet they were sincere: this was where they were meant to be.

"It was such a mistake," said their leader Arixys. "Our fathers and mothers left in such high hopes, convinced that it was the right thing to do. Many of the settlers didn't really understand the fate of the leftovers ... of you all. And those that did told themselves that it was all for the best, that they had no choice.

"It was not hard to forget. Our homes were so amazing. The food, the views, the culture and life, everything was incredible. The original settlers were soon having children. We didn't know anything else, growing up. We thought it was all just normal.

"But somehow it drifted. There was a, a lack? A lost connection? We tried filling it with music, with sex, even with religion. But we just felt empty. Like our brains were stitched too loosely to the insides of our skulls.

"Philosophers tried to explain it; psychologists tried to ease it; most of us tried to forget it. But over time, people just stopped caring. One by one, they gave up dance, theater, then conversation, food. They stopped sleeping, stopped drinking, and eventually, just lay down and died. We talked to them, of course, but no-one could tell us why. There didn't seem to be anything wrong, exactly; more like nothing was right.

"It was not just one or two people, not just certain families or sectors. It was all over, catching on like a contagion. It became clear that this was a threat to our survival. It was consuming us, so that almost before we knew it, our population was disappearing. We had to do something.

"Then it came for my father, Edgar. To everyone else he was this guru, but to me he was just my dad. He wore white and lit incense and chanted. But that was nothing special, it was all I knew.

"I hated him for a long time, you know. He basically kidnapped me and dragged me along on his ridiculous adventure. I was too young to understand. He'd keep droning on about possibilities and how wonderful everything would be. I was just like, I have no idea what is happening. But he was so desperate to see the glass half full.

"Here, I kept them, these letters." They pulled a packet of papers out and handed it to the survivors. "While he was off getting ready for the ascension or whatever, I was left alone. We had to write old-style, for security. Read them if you like. I guess they're the only real history we have.

"As I grew older, the whole thing, yeah, it was amazing. Really. I never lacked for anything in Earth-2. But we always had this guilt, we could never quite forget what we had done, how we had left you all behind. Every time we saw the sun, we knew, somehow we knew what lay behind it. The crimes hidden on the far side of the sun. It tainted everything that we touched and everything that we did. Edgar was way overcompensating, it was a bit pathetic actually. He was always going on about renewal and moving on, about leaving the past behind and creating a new tomorrow. Blah blah blah. I stopped hating him and started pitying him.

"But then the half glass got fully empty, I guess. He just stopped one day, said he couldn't see the point. They used to come to him for counsel, but when he needed help, there was no-one there. Not me, that's for sure. I mean, I tried to get him up, make him show an interest, but nothing changed. Soon enough, he was just lying there, dying of disaffect. And I could feel it creeping into me as well. It's hard to motivate someone to change when, deep down, you kind of envy them.

"While everyone was looking for medical or psychological expla-nations, I wondered, 'What if this is spiritual?' My father had been chosen as one of the spiritual leaders of the new world. But for us, 'spiritual' meant some yoga classes, some nice mindfulness sessions. The big questions—Why are we here? Who are we? What does it mean to be awake?—they all seemed a little morbid. But with so much going so wrong, maybe there was something we'd missed?

"I looked into the spiritual classics of the past—*Walden*,

The Bible, The Dhammapada, Zen and the Art of Motorcycle Main-tenance—and noticed a theme. There was something about a connection with place. With the earth. There seemed something subtle that we'd lost. Perhaps it was so pervasive that no-one noticed it. One day I came across a collection of stories by Indigenous Australians. It was a book of tales told for children, with bright pictures of talking animals. But I knew that there was a depth there. The stories spoke of how their life was bound up with their land in ways that could not be fathomed by science.

"I began to wonder, 'Could we be dying of homesickness? Could it be that we have cut some fundamental tether, that our being is in some mysterious way bound up with the being of the earth? Of *this* earth that is. That our lives simply cannot exist without our Mother?' "

They paused for a moment to collect themself. Katy nodded, "Yeah, makes sense. It's home. This thin layer of slime on a ball of rock. It's country."

Arixys continued. "I began to work on getting back. It seemed like our only hope. The ships that had brought us were still there in orbit. When I began, everyone scoffed and sneered. But as I was getting the ships ready for a return journey, they kept dying. I was too late to save my dad. By the time I was ready, everyone, the entire remaining population of Earth-2, wanted a place. And I gave it them. Here we are, the final remnants of humanity's greatest folly: the idea that we could have anything we wanted. And that we would never have to pay the price."

And so they stayed, all twenty-seven of them. There was no lack of space. They seemed to find a measure of peace, a sense of reconciliation, in their time back home on Earth-1, as they called it. But it was not long. Was it the ashen lungs, the bitter, oily water, some unseen disease, or simply the searing sun on tender pink flesh? Within a few weeks they were gone. And so ended the great experiment.

One by one, the survivors passed as well. They had been happy enough, content together in the end of days. They had done for each other, had a few laughs now and then. But life was tough, and every year it got tougher. Her father, Dr. Chris, disappeared one day, they never knew where. They just woke up and he was gone. He'd always been a bit of a loner.

Her mother regretted often, she knew, her choice to have a child. It was the hardest thing she'd done, and many times it had almost killed her. But here she was. And it was okay. Her mother always said that Eliana was the only good thing to come out of all this.

Until she lay dying, with her daughter beside her, stroking her face. "Eliana," she said softly, "listen. You have to leave this place." Their home in Parramatta was over, they knew that. The seas were rising. The ground had become treacherous, the buildings were sinking underfoot and above, breaking in the storms.

"But where to go, amma?"

"There's a palace," she whispered. "in the hills. It's beautiful. I never found it. But you can."

"What palace, amma? Where do I find it?"

Sharon never spoke again. Eliana made a bed of lilies for her, with a pillow of rose.

Why had the white people come here and not to some more flourishing remnant? The survivors had always imagined that somewhere things wouldn't be quite so bad. There must be villages, towns, communities adapting and thriving in all kinds of ways. After all, the earth was broad.

But Arixys had said no. "We scanned the surface; it was the same technology that was used to survey Earth-2. There's nothing. After the fires, the plagues, the floods, the nukes ..."

"Wait," said Leslie, "there's nukes now?"

"Yes," said Arixys, "multiple cities were bombed. It appears there was localized nuclear conflict in several arenas."

"Oh," said Leslie pensively. "It just feels like we ought to have known."

Everywhere, on earth and in space, only one human settlement remained, their little tribe in the ruins of the City of Parramatta.

And now that was gone and there was just her and Norm.

The memories of story didn't offer much in the way of directions. She was really just walking at random. Let her feet find the way. Onwards and upwards, that was her only map. But they were high now, higher than the city. Instead of ruined buildings around them, it was ruined bush. Mostly ash and rock. No more broken homes to raid. There were gullies, somewhat sheltered, where some berries might be scrounged, or a root dug up.

They were slowly dying, but what else was new?

One day—a couple of weeks after setting out? Who knows?—it was just as the dawn was rising, she saw a flash of yellow on the ground, up to the right. She was walking along what had once been a path. The haze was strong, everything was blanked out after about five meters or so. The ground, everything she could see was a dull neutral gray. But that yellow popped and she stepped over to it. It was a piece of plastic, a wrapper for junk food. *Twisties* it said, the red logo bright against the yellow. She was strangely arrested by the sight. It wasn't that it was so unusual. True, most of the loose plastic had disintegrated by then, turned to microparticles, part of the haze that was everywhere and in everything, including her own flesh. But there was still a fair bit around here and there, raggedy and worn. Anyway, there it was, colorful and cheerful, almost brazen: "Here I am, apocalypse. Take that!"

She wondered who had made it. She knew it came from a factory, not that she'd ever seen one, but she was familiar with the concept. Lots of metal machines, all making the same exact thing, thousands and millions of them, sent out into the world to amuse and destroy.

But someone must have said, "Let's make it bright yellow, so it really stands out! Let's make it *that* shade of yellow, that exact shade." Out of all the millions of colors. How did they work those things out? Did someone just draw it, or was there a committee who decided? Someone somewhere thought it was such a good idea: a happy color, grab your attention. They must have been stoked when their idea made it out into the world! When the first packet of Twisties came out of the factory, they would have been thrilled! She imagined them going to the shop and proudly buying a packet, beaming, saying to everyone, "See, that yellow? That's my color!" And they'd all laugh and cheer and eat Twisties together. She had no idea how they tasted, but it must have been something special. And that color had lasted all these years. But now the factory was gone, the company was gone, the one who chose the yellow was gone, and there was no-one left alive to remember the taste of Twisties.

Drawn by the yellow, she turned upwards and to the right, pressing on once more. The Twisties packet stayed behind, slowly crumbling into soil and air. Norm nuzzled the packet and licked it, but was disappointed: it didn't taste of anything. So he lost interest and ran off leaving it to decay. It was only natural.

The air became a little softer and Norm, ever alert, pricked up his nose. They were edging their way along a gully, a wall of sandstone to their right. There, just visible, was a dark patch, like a smudge. She exchanged a look with Norm; they thought it worth checking out. Picking their way with their slow, sure feet, they came near the rocks. It was all overgrown with thorns, but behind there was an opening.

It was clear. The floor was flat, it looked man-made, but covered all over with soft white sand. They stepped inside, their footprints marking the pristine surface; not many animals about. The roof arched a few meters, easily high enough to walk upright. The sun had risen behind them, shining in the entrance, so they could see in a little. The walls disappeared off either side, maybe a dozen paces across. There was a bit of rubble and junk; it had been occupied at some point.

As their eyes got used to the dark, she turned and saw something looming. It looked strange, like a huge figure. Coming closer, she saw it was a statue, carved into the rock. A man sitting. More than man-height. He looked somehow peaceful. The rock was melting, the features blurring as the soft sandstone crumbled away. But it was still clear enough; the crumbling made it somehow even more still, like a moment caught in stasis.

It exerted a strange power over her. She sat in front of it, adopting its cross-legged posture in the soft cool sand. Norm lay down beside her. She had heard Arixys talk about what he called "meditation".

He said they practiced a thing called "mindfulness", but she never really got it. To be aware, in your body, in the present? Where else would you be? For her, awareness wasn't a "practice", it was her life. In the apocalypse, if you weren't present, you were dead. A bite, a scratch, the wrong kind of berry. Anything at all could kill you, and it probably would. She had learned this from her ammas: silence, care with every step, awareness of every sound, attunement to her own breathing. That was her education; it was what kept her alive when everything else was dead.

Now, for the first time, she tried to actually "meditate" as a practice. It was a bit weird and uncomfortable at first. She closed her eyes and reached out for her breath. It rose and fell, slowly, rhythmically. But oddly, the more she tried to concentrate on it, the tighter it grew, and the slipperier. It was full of tension and crags. She could feel her fear in it. So she eased off and let her breath come to her. It washed over her like a tide or a hug. It caressed her, soothing and loving. It was life, and it had been with her since the day she was born. She didn't have to concentrate on it, just let it take care of her.

The rhythms, energies, and tensions in her body were gently soothed away. She noticed, it had inside it a pleasure. Something deep and ecstatic, almost like a syrup soaking through her. Where had this been all her life, she wondered? Tears welled gently in her eyes. A word rose to her that she'd never heard: *caber-ra nanga*. It seemed to fit.

The pleasure and the peace drew her inwards. The weight and burden of her body lifted. Her breath changed, glowing softly from inside itself. A tender joy arose as if from nowhere, as if it had been there all along. She could hear, just, Norm whimpering like he always did. But the light became stronger. It went on for a long time. It came and went but slowly, slowly drew her deeper.

Until inside, as it were, the tenderness, the grief that she felt for her mother, for her family, for the whole world, it came up from deep and poured out in a river of tears. Norm didn't like that, not one bit; he stood and licked the tears away. She kept going, through grief into anger, resentment, and despair. Everything that had been locked away for so many years came up and into her. She was surging, bourne up on a vast wave of pain. So much loss, so much loss! Oceans of tears, numberless. It was too much! The ghosts of a billion wasted lives howled within her, begging for vengeance and atonement.

How could she bear it, so thin and frail? How could she bear so much pain? Men used to tell little girls like her that they were weak, fragile creatures, too delicate for the harsh things of the world. But now those men were dust and there was no-one to tell her she was weak. So she stayed.

She rocked back and forth, wailing, insensible to all but the suffering. Still it kept on, wave after wave of despair, a mountain crushing souls like ants.

She stayed. She was tough as hell. She'd beaten the apocalypse, hadn't she?

She stayed. And eventually, she came through. Her breath came back. The light came back. For a moment, she thought it was daylight and opened her eyes. But she had been sitting for many hours; night had fallen and it was utterly black inside the cave. She closed her eyes again and bathed in the light of her breath. The light grew and grew, the power in her mind grew and grew, until of a sudden, it opened up and she fell into it. It was as if there was a part of her, a part that she had been holding on to her whole life, but had never known existed; and it just wasn't there any more.

She stepped out of this world and into another.

In that other world there was only light and bliss and love and freedom. There was no doubt, no pain. She was more aware, more awake than she'd ever been; yet she couldn't see or hear or feel. It was unlike anything she had ever imagined, but it felt totally natural. It felt like coming home. Time had stopped, and thought and movement and wishing. There was only an eternity of bliss, as if the present had stretched out to cover the whole universe.

After a long while, eternity came to an end. Her mind drew back from the present, and she stretched it out to encompass the past. She traced back the steps that had brought her here, her journey, her home in the ruins of Parramatta; her ammas, their death, and their lives; the brief interlude with the white folk from the stars. She saw back to her childhood, wading in the water looking for yams, then further to her fiery birth. Then there was a veil; the end of the known. She could see no further. But still, she reached out with her mind, poking at the veil until, to her surprise, it shimmered and gave way; and there she saw something strange and mysterious: her consciousness emerging inside the womb. A beating spark, an embryo of knowing, arising in sheer darkness. But no, it wasn't just dark; there was something else there; a cord, a conduit of light leading out of this life.

She followed the conduit and emerged, startled, in another life. Like a vision of another world, she saw. She was on a street, a busy street, tall buildings shining in the sun. It was unrecognizable, but she knew it was her own place, the town square of Parramatta. She was sitting at a table eating—oh! It was so delicious! Flaky, crusty, and sweet, like nothing she had tasted. She had freckles and big red hair and a faded denim jacket with studs like stars and she was laughing with her friends; and she had a name: Michelle. Her heart was full of love.

Then further back, to another life. Roger. An apprentice, also there in Parramatta. He was a mechanic, covered in grease. No fancy café pastries for him, he ate a sausage roll and shared a beer with his mates, listening to rock-n-roll on the radio. It blasted "Tutti Frutti, aw rooty" and one of the guys spat out, "What's this 'fruity' shit?" He shared a sly glance with one of his mates and said, "I dunno, sounds hot to me."

And again, back. Oh! This was loud, full of guns and explosions! She was in a tent, a big green dim tent, with beds ... a hospital. It was war. She was young, a nurse, her name was Keiko. She saw the people. They spoke a language she had never heard, but she understood. On the side of the tent was a flag: red sun on white background. In front of her was a young man on a bed screaming. But she was not afraid. And a whistle as the bombs came down and it all went black.

And back again she went. This time she was in a small shed, tin walls and roof, and it was hot. Phew, so hot! She was standing at the front talking and sweating, her name was Mary; her hair was severe grey but her dress had flowers. She was a teacher. In front of her was a room full of little Noongar kids sitting at their desks. She was trying not to laugh at something naughty one of them had done. Through the window, bright sun and blue sky and gum trees waving.

162

And again, back, and again. Life after life after life, she saw it unfolding. She knew, she knew, at last she knew! This was what life was, what it could be, what it was no longer.

She turned from the past to see the roads leading to possible futures. She saw, this is where they had gone. This is how they had lived, what they had chosen, and this where their choices were leading.

She saw them all, the ghosts that surrounded her. The bewildered spirits of the past wailing in grief and confusion. She knew: this is what happened to them after they died. They had lived lives of plenty, had enjoyed what might be enjoyed and suffered what must be suffered. They had breathed the air with no thought for the future, had eaten and made love and got drunk and forgotten. They had forgotten all the tomorrows. They had laughed and laughed, thinking they had all the answers.

Now they were the forgotten ones, living in their own forgotten tomorrows, their future stretching out before them like a wasted land. Caught in-between, not condemned to torment, nor raised up to bliss, they were just lost, so lost, so lonely. They were lost but they were not gone. Lost in the space between the worlds, they could not move on.

They shuffled in their restless hordes, lamenting the world of ruin that was their birthright and their legacy. They keened strange cries, nonsensical relics of broken language that had long outlived their purpose: "Electoral suicide!" "Gas-fired recovery!" "Tech not taxes!" Their world of shades was incomprehensible to them; they could not understand why it was the way it was. One fact only burned bright and sure in their minds: they were guilty and it was too late.

This was all they would ever know, this their only home, this what they truly deserved: the acid and wretched decay of ruination and despair, lost and lamenting as the long hours of their days crumbled slowly into dust. There was to be no redemption for them, no forgiveness, and no atonement. Only an age of desolation until the wages of their deeds were utterly spent; so that, released at last from the prison in which they had trapped themselves, they might move on to whatever fate awaited them next. A new life, perhaps, with a chance to make better choices.

She saw it all and she knew. She knew.

Like all things good or ill, her meditation came to an end. She felt herself coming back into her body, her senses waking up, clawing and scratching their way back into consciousness. Even in that dark space the light was startling. Painful, but not strong pain like when you step into the sun, something more subtle. Her skin wrapped around her like an octopus.

It was weird; on the one hand, she felt so peaceful and happy, basking in the afterglow of her deep meditation and realization. Hunger and fatigue were gone, and her body was light and soft like cotton wool. On the other hand, there was an ever-so-subtle underlying sense that something was just wrong. She wondered about that. Bliss lived inside her mind, she knew that now. All the pain and suffering, the death of a trillion sentient beings, that was such a small thing, a shadow cast by the world of bliss. Or perhaps the bliss was simply the space that opened up on the far side of pain.

She caught up some sand and looked at it. It was as if she was seeing things for the first time. She rubbed the sand, feeling its texture, letting it run through her fingers. She thought back to the ocean of grief, and she realized: "All that pain, all that loss, all that is falling in this sand. And that bliss is falling alongside it." The huge hilarious tragedy that they called "humanity" seemed like a distant star, blinking. What was past and what was to come folded into the present, and the present dried up and blew away in the wind.

Like a sigh, she knew. Everything that has a beginning must have an end. All this pain, all this suffering—it is exactly what it seems. The final bonds in her heart fell away, dissolving like cobwebs in the wind, leaving nothing behind but peace. Her mind went out like a flame.

What once had been Eliana's body remained seated while Norm lay down beside it, patiently waiting. After a while he grew hungry. He sniffed at the body, sitting so very still and lifeless. Slobbering, he gave it a lick. The skin was salty and nice. Now he was even hungrier. It was only natural.

epilogue

Upon the ship's prow the Commander proudly stood, their voice ringing clear over the shining waters of the bay: "One, two, three—heave! One, two, three—heave!" The workers were tired, but they gave it their all. And then, it moved! Revived, they pulled all the harder.

The Commander rushed to the boat's side and peered intently. In the bright clear waters they could discern the object breaking free of the sandy floor far below, sending eels darkly scattering. The workers hauled it up from the deep—through flashing silver of fish, through seaweed waving freshly green—until there, at the end of the rope, the mysterious shape took form. When it broke free of the brilliant waters, it did not disappoint: a golden pillar, tall and unbent, finely decorated with arcane carvings. The royal Treasurer hurried to inspect it, their careful eye confirming its authenticity and value.

Together the Commander and the Treasurer brought the news to the Monarch Sankha, who was seated upon the sea-shell throne in the great palace. Sankha rose from the throne and cried out, "May the peace of Mahāpanāda be upon you all! Let us declare a great offering!"

The court rejoiced and set to work. The kitchens busied themselves, the yard was cleared, pavilions were set up. In the morning, a messenger was sent to the monastery to issue the invitation.

The monastery was situated in the land once known as Balmoral, on a soft rise by the shore of the bay, looking out over the harbor towards the narrow cliff-bound entrance. The sky was piercing blue, the sun warm and gentle. In the cool shade of tall trees there sat the Buddha whose name was Maitreya, surrounded by noble and peaceful mendicants. Each one of them was clad in a simple yellow robe, content and devoted to a life of harmlessness.

The messenger approached the Buddha, paid respects, and said, "O honored one, the Monarch has invited you for a meal. They wish to celebrate the discovery of the golden pillar of the Wheel-Turning Monarch Mahāpanāda." The Buddha consented in silence. When the messenger had left, the Buddha stood and arranged their robe. Then, taking their bowl, they left for the palace with a large retinue. They walked barefoot and mindful along the soft, grassy pathways through bushland adorned with flowers of every color. Birdsong was their herald, and all around them, beasts of the forest slowly gathered, escorting them along their way.

The Monarch received them and invited the Buddha to a seat of honor. Before the court, flanked by the Commander and the Treasurer, they declared, "O honored one, we have raised up the pillar of the Wheel-Turning Monarch Mahāpanāda. It is a sign! Mahāpanāda, it is said, established a rich and prosperous realm. There was wealth and plenty unimaginable. Now under my rule we shall flourish once more! In days past such an event would have been marked with a

168

cruel sacrifice, the slaughter of a horse. But now that I have encountered the Dhamma, I have rejected such practices. Instead, I invite you to share the meal together with your community."

"It is well," replied the Buddha. "But know this: this is not the first time that such a realm of prosperity has arisen. One day, many long years in the past, there were people in this same land who attained to a level of wealth that surpassed even that of Mahāpanāda."

And they told a story of the past.

> "Between the mountains and the sea there lay a wide
> valley by a narrow river. There the salt water mixed
> with the fresh and eels born in distant seas came to lie
> down in the mangroves. ... It was only natural."

At the end, they identified the birth. "You might think that someone else was Norm the faithful hound in those days. But do not think so. It was I myself who accompanied Eliana on their last journey. And at that time, the Commander was known as Katy, while the Treasurer was Leslie. And you, O Monarch Sankha, were none other than Sharon, the wise and just leader of the last humans on Earth of old.

"And now I say to you: in those days past, happiness came from letting go and contentment, and so it is today. The gold and pomp you love so much will end in dust. Your only protection is your good deeds, and your only true sanctuary is peace."

The monarch was so moved that, after offering the meal, they called a great gathering of their citizens under the pillar of Mahāpanāda. There they distributed all their wealth to their people, reserving only an extra gold coin for each of the workers. Then, after ensuring that each worker was paid for their trouble, they issued a final instruction.

"Take the golden pillar," said the Monarch, "and cast it back into the sea! I shall no longer live trapped by the lure of shiny things."

They renounced the throne and went forth to live as a mendicant under the guidance of the Buddha Maitreya. The Commander and the Treasurer renounced as well, and together they set out to seek liberation.

timeline

- circa 360–300 million BCE: Most of the world's coal is formed.
- circa 60,000+ BCE: Australia is settled by First Peoples.
- circa 2900 BCE: Gilgamesh logs the cedar forests.
- circa 400 BCE: Indian sage Siddhattha Gotama, the Buddha, speaks of anthropogenic climate change. Global atmospheric CO2 is about 278 ppm.
- 1687: Isaac Newton's *Philosophiæ Naturalis Principia Mathematica* lays the foundation for modern science.
- 1712: Thomas Newcomen's "atmospheric engine", the first effective coal-powered steam engine, ushers in an age of unprecedented economic growth and technological progress.
- 1770: Isaac Smith, a crew member on Captain Cook's *Endeavour*, becomes the first white man to set foot in Australia, trespassing on the land of the Gweagal people at the place called by them Kamay and by the English Botany Bay.
- 1824: French physicist Joseph Fourier describes the Earth's natural "greenhouse effect".
- 1856: U.S. scientist Eunice Foote experimentally proves the heat-absorbing properties of CO2. Her findings are confirmed

in 1861 by John Tyndall.

- 1896: Swedish chemist Svante Arrhenius posits that coal burning will amplify the greenhouse effect, raising temperatures by several degrees.
- 1938: British engineer Guy Callendar confirms that temperatures had been rising over the past century, and hypothesizes that rising CO2 is the cause.
- 1957: Discovery of Earth-2.
- 1958: Charles Keeling begins measurement of CO2 at Mauna Loa. It is 315.70 ppm.
- 1965 / 320 ppm: A report to the White House by the President's Science Advisory Committee warns: "Throughout his worldwide industrial civilization, Man is unwittingly conducting a vast geophysical experiment. Within a few generations he is burning the fossil fuels that slowly accumulated in the earth over the past 500 million years."
- 1980–2030: Building Earth-2.
- 1981 / 340 ppm: Secret global warming report to Australian Prime Minister Malcolm Fraser warns of the threat to Australia's coal revenues.
- 1989 / 353 ppm: UK Prime Minister Margaret Thatcher warns: "Change in future is likely to be more fundamental and more widespread than anything we have known hitherto."
- 1992 / 356 ppm: Rio de Janeiro Earth Summit, the first international attempt to reach a global consensus to stop global warming.
- 1996 / 362 ppm: Birth of Dr. Chris.
- 2001 / 371 ppm: Birth of Leslie & Other Chris.

- 2006 / 382 ppm: Birth of Sharon.
- 2007 / 384 ppm: Australian Prime Minister Kevin Rudd declares climate change is "the great moral challenge of our time".
- 2008 / 385 ppm: Birth of Katy.
- 2009 / 387 ppm: Soon-to-be Australian Prime Minister Tony Abbott declares climate change is "absolute crap".
- 2010 / 390 ppm: Birth of Arixys.
- 2020 / 414 ppm: Pandemic & fires are the new normal.
- 2021 / 416 ppm: Global atmospheric CO_2 continues to rise at an accelerating rate.
- 2022: Other Chris loses his wife.
- 2023: Edgar writes to his son Arixys, prepares for Departure.
- 2024: Sharon loses her home, Australia declares martial law.
- 2025: The Departure. Katy leaves home.
- 2026: Katy and Sharon, and soon after Leslie, meet up and form the Harbingers.
- 2030: General collapse of civilization. Billions die.
- 2034: The two Chrises meet.
- 2036: Chrises meet Harbingers.
- 2040: Birth of Eliana.
- 2049: The Return.
- 2058: Survivors are all dead. Eliana awakens.
- 2063: Global atmospheric CO_2 exceeds 600 ppm, but no-one is alive to measure it.
- 5,932,786,291 / 278 ppm: The pillar of King Mahāpanāda is retrieved.

www.ingramcontent.com/pod-product-compliance
Lightning Source LLC
Chambersburg PA
CBHW020121180626
46812CB00006B/2692